ZOE'S
BLOCKADE

Destiny's Trinities
▲ *Book 5* ▲

TRACY
COOPER-POSEY

STORIES RULE
EDMONTON • ALBERTA

This is an original publication of Tracy Cooper-Posey

This is a work of fiction. Names, characters, places and incidents either are the product of the author's imagination or are used fictitiously, and any resemblance to actual persons, living or dead, business establishments, events, or locales, is entirely coincidental. The publisher does not have any control over and does not assume any responsibility for third-party websites or their content.

Copyright © 2016 by Tracy Cooper-Posey
Text design by Tracy Cooper-Posey

Cover by Dar Albert
Wicked Smart Designs
http://WickedSmartDesigns.com

Edited by Helen Woodall
http://HelenWoodallFreelanceEditing.blogspot.com/

FIRST EDITION: July 2016

Cooper-Posey, Tracy
Zoe's Blockade/Tracy Cooper-Posey—1st Ed.

Romance—Fiction
Paranormal – Fiction

Chapter One

"I gotta be somewhere near the north pole by now," Diego groused. "I feel as if I've been driving for a century." He paused to steer the Mustang around a deep curve of the road, which was hugging a monster outcrop of rock, using both hands on the wheel.

"You didn't learn how to drive until last year," Blake pointed out. His voice emerging from the car speakers sounded reasonable and calm. "It'll be a while before you catch up."

"You can't possibly be near the north pole yet," Sera said, her voice as serene as always. Even though she was in Florida, she sounded louder and clearer than Blake, who was sitting at his desk in New York.

Diego gritted his jaw against the emptiness in his chest that always made itself felt whenever he was talking to them. "I miss you guys," he breathed.

"You have to find your trinity soon," Blake assured him, his voice dropping in volume. He was trying to avoid being overheard. "Where are you, anyway?"

Diego saw a big green sign coming up. "Hang on," he

said and waited for the lettering to be clear enough to read. "Revelstoke."

"Still in British Columbia, then," Blake said.

"Revelstoke in the Rockies, isn't it?" Sera said. "I'm looking at a map now. It must be beautiful."

"Beautifully white and boring," Diego muttered. "The bloody snow is already a foot thick around here and it's only October."

"Oh! It sounds wonderful!" Sera breathed. "There are trees, too, yes?"

"You be careful, driving in that stuff," Blake added.

"Yes, lieutenant."

"I mean it. In driving terms, you're every cop's nightmare. You've been driving just long enough to think you're great at it and not long enough to know how to get yourself out of trouble when it happens."

Diego gritted his teeth together.

"He's scolding because he loves you," Sera said, only this time it was from right next to him. She was sitting in the passenger seat.

Diego jumped. "Mary, mother of God and all her saints! Sera! What the fuck?"

She smiled at him, her big eyes wide.

"What? She's there?" Blake asked.

"Yes," Diego breathed. He felt winded. "Sera, I'm going way too fast for you to try that sort of stunt. You've never seen this place, you have no idea what you were jumping to. Of all the stupid...."

"And now *he's* scolding because he loves you," Blake said.

Sera's smile was complacent. "Yet despite all the risks, here I sit." She looked at the mountain peaks around them, completely covered in snow. The endless march of fir trees, the only color in the landscape anywhere. "It *is* beautiful," she declared.

Diego had to admit that she was right. The farther north he'd gotten, the more spectacular the scenery had become. At times he regretted having to concentrate on driving. He would have enjoyed stopping to look around, only the urge to keep going, to keep seeking, had been pushing him onward for a week now.

He had flown to Seattle and rented the Mustang there, then started north, crossing into Canada late that afternoon.

Why he had come this way, he didn't know. He'd learned from the others that the impulse to seek out their trinity didn't arrive with maps and directions. He had to follow his gut. Well, he had been doing that for centuries, so it was no burden. Although it *was* boring.

He braked, slowing. Then he dropped the speed by changing down the gears, easing it to a slow stop. He'd learned quickly that stamping on the brakes could send the little sports car into a heart-squeezing fishtail on these icy roads.

"What's wrong?" Sera asked.

"I don't know."

"What's happening?" Blake asked.

"Diego is stopping," Sera said.

He brought the car to a final halt, pulling off the cleared section of the road into the inch of snow carpeting the edges, dropped the car into neutral and put on the handbrake. He looked at Sera, in her skimpy tank top and cotton skirt. "Stay in the car. It's only fifteen degrees out there."

As he opened the door, she wrapped her arms around herself and shivered.

He shut the door and did a slow full circle, taking in everything. Had the direction changed? *Something* had forced him to stop.

His breath came out in thick, steamy billows, so he stopped breathing. Then he held still, put his head down and eased his senses out to their maximum and waited.

There. From over there.

He lifted his head and looked in the direction he felt the urge to go. It was off the road, up against the base of a mountain range. A thick batch of trees hid all other detail.

He strained his vision to the utmost and saw that the green swathes were broken up by a structure. He glimpsed white, too. More snow, which meant open areas. A house?

Diego got back into the car and pulled warm air into his

lungs. He put the car back in gear and drove slowly along the road, looking for a side road to appear. "Somewhere on the left, up there," he told Sera.

"Among those trees?"

"Think so." The compulsion was growing stronger now. Except it wasn't the only thing building in his mind.

"I can feel blackness ahead," Sera murmured, her voice strained.

"Still there, Blake?" Diego asked.

"I've got Google Maps up. I can see where you might be. There's nothing on the map around there."

"Private house," Diego muttered. The darkness in his head was growing thicker. "I think we might have company, too," he added.

"Grimoré?"

"Or vampeen. That trinity over in Pennsylvania figured out that the Grimoré were using forests to farm the vampeen. Maybe it's the same here."

"In the snow?"

"It's not that cold," Diego protested.

"Says the vampire who can't feel anything," Blake replied.

"I can feel it," Sera said. "The cold *and* the black."

"Sera, jump back out of there," Blake said sharply.

"I can fight," Sera said firmly. "Diego is on his own."

"Then jump back here and get me and *I'll* help him,"

7

Blake said. "You don't have a weapon."

"Diego has two guns," Sera pointed out.

Diego shook his head. "I had to leave them behind. International border and this is Canada. You can't carry guns around, even if you can get a permit."

Sera bit her lip. "Then what are you going to do? Blake, I can come and get yours."

"You don't even have a knife, Diego? What the hell?" Blake said, sounding pissed. "Sera, jump back to the apartment, you can get his spares."

"No, no time," Diego said. "Hold on."

He turned into the side route that had appeared. It was a gravel road, well ploughed and clear of snow. White fencing and two wagon wheels propped on either side for decoration told him this was private property. Beyond the fenced opening, they plunged into a tree-lined tunnel with pale blue sky for a roof.

From the corner of his eye, Diego could see movement through the trees on either side of the car. Flashes of something moving at speed. Matching them.

Sera gripped the armrest, her knuckles white. "There's something out there," she whispered.

"Don't stop," Blake said, his voice quiet. He liked to give orders and constantly fussed about safety and security, only when the real fight was about to begin, he turned into the hunter he really was—wary and short on conversation.

"Sera, jump back to Blake," Diego said tersely.

"No."

He hissed his frustration, but didn't try again. Sera wouldn't leave until he was safe, now.

Instead, he settled down to drive the car as fast as he could on the narrow route. That wasn't fast at all and whatever it was out there, it was keeping pace with them. That meant it probably wasn't vampeen, who started off life as human. No human could run as fast as a car, even a car dipping into every little pothole and bumping along a country road. It just wasn't physically possible.

Yet he could *feel* vampeen. Out here, where there were no other sentient signatures and traces to confuse the markers, the sense that the vampeen were nearby was almost screaming at him.

"A bridge," Sera said and pointed ahead.

The trees were broken up by a small ravine. A bridge of steel grids crossed it. The average bridge was slippery, Diego had learned. This metal one would be even more icy.

The shadows flashing through the trees alongside them were coming closer. They were big and low to the ground.

Diego gripped the wheel. "Hold on," he said shortly. "They're coming for us."

"Can they stop a car?" Sera asked, her voice high.

"I don't know. I don't know what they are."

The things broke through the trees and leapt at the car.

They looked like really big dogs. Larger than wolves. Their eyes were red. The teeth in their snapping, drooling jaws were the same as the familiar vampeen—crossed, crooked, sharp and deadly.

The lead dog rammed into the side of the car, rocking it and cracking the glass in the passenger door next to Sera's shoulder. She muffled a scream against her hand. Diego fought the wheel, keeping the car steady and keeping it moving forward.

More of the dog-things launched at them. Claws scraped the sides of the car, making the metal scream. They brushed up against the side of it and Diego felt the rear wobble, threatening to fishtail. If they spun out, they would be lost.

He stamped on the gas and the car straightened up. They were going way too fast, now. If he hit ice, he would have no control at all.

The bridge was just ahead.

Three of the dog creatures were standing shoulder to shoulder in front of the bridge. Guarding it.

They were snarling, audible over the noise of the car engine and the growling of the other dogs around the car. One of them pawed the ground. They all looked ready to spring.

"Jump, Sera!" Diego shouted.

Instead she lifted her arm to shield her face and turned her head away from the windshield.

Diego slammed into the creatures. The Mustang was a

small car and low to the ground. The heavy engine at the front weighed it down, keeping it stable.

The middle creature flipped over the hood of the car, thudded against the windshield, which starred and bowed in the middle, but didn't break. The creature was thrown over the roof. The other two were hammered aside by the corners of the car.

The Mustang shot forward onto the steel grid work of the bridge. The rear wiggled, then shifted some more…and kept turning.

The car began to spin. The rear slammed into the low steel girders protecting the sides of the bridge and bounced back. On the icy deck, the tires couldn't grip. The driver's side of the car ricocheted off the girder. By that time the front wheels were off the bridge deck and back onto gravel, which offered only slightly more grip. It was enough to anchor the wheels, sending the back of the car into a complete spin.

Diego turned the wheel, cranking it, trying to steer into the spin and halt it. They didn't have enough speed to compensate. The car drifted into a full four-wheel spin, coming to a stop twenty yards beyond the bridge. The engine cut out.

The silence was broken only by the non-canine growling of the dogs, back on the other side of the bridge. They were making no attempt to cross the bridge.

"Hell's hounds!" Diego swore. He looked at Sera. "Are you all right?"

She nodded. "Is that what they are? Hell Hounds?"

Diego shook his head. "Hell hounds are meaner and faster. These are creatures of the vampeen."

"They're guarding the bridge. Stopping anyone from coming or going," Sera said. She looked through the cracked window next to her. "They're halting whoever lives there from leaving," she added.

Diego dipped his head to look through the window where the cracks and starring didn't block the view. There was a ranch house ahead. It was made of logs, although it bore little relationship to the rustic log cabins of yore. There were two levels and a third attic level with dormer windows thrusting from the sharp-pitched roof, hidden beneath a thick layer of snow despite the slope. Heavy posts held up verandahs on both levels.

There was a big Ford Explorer sitting on the gravel in front of the house. It was empty.

"I guess I'd better go and give them the good news," Diego said.

Sera studied the house, biting her lip. "Is that the place, Diego? Is that the trinity?"

"Even if I wasn't certain it was the place, the vampeen make it a lock." He looked around. "They're probably waiting for low light to make a move. They're as drawn to the forming trinity as I am." He looked Sera over once more, checking her for wounds. She was as pretty and untouched as always, her crystalline blue eyes calm.

"The call to Blake got dropped in all the excitement," he told her. "You'd better jump back there and tell him what happened or he'll be on the first flight out here to find out for himself."

She nodded. "Beth, too. She needs to know about the hounds." She leaned over the console and kissed him. "Be careful, Diego."

"For you, I'll try."

She gave him a smile, the little one that promised much. Then she was gone.

Diego started the car. It ran choppily. Something was fatally wrong with it. It would get him to the house and that was all he needed for now. He glanced at the hounds once more. They still made no attempt to draw closer, even when he pulled the nose of the car around to face the house. They seemed to be content to bar access over the bridge.

"Let there be another way out of here," Diego breathed.

Chapter Two

Zoe paused, the kettle lifted over the French press, listening. Had she heard dogs? When she heard nothing more except for the caw of the big crow that liked sit on the powerlines outside the window, she started pouring the water again. Cole would be down soon. She wanted to have the coffee ready when he padded into the kitchen. He had been out late last night, dealing with a group of winter campers on the lower slopes of Mt. MacPherson.

As she was fitting the lid to the pot, she heard the clatter of a car engine approaching the house. It was a very sick car, from the sound of it. Someone on the Trans-Canada highway had obviously gotten into mechanical trouble and had pulled into the house for help. It was a dumb move. They were only five miles away from Revelstoke here. The car could have made it to the town just as easily as negotiating the rutted road from the highway. Although Zoe had learned that city-based tourists weren't used to thinking those ways.

With a silent sigh, she moved through the house to the front door, shoved her snow boots and heavy parka on, then stepped out onto the verandah. The freezing air washed over her.

The first sight of the car made her heart give a little flutter of unease. It was a late model Mustang. The windshield had been busted in and there were heavy dents in the hood. Had he hit a deer? Deer would do that sort of damage on a low car.

The Mustang pulled up next to Cole's truck and the driver got out. Dark hair, olive skin, eyes that looked as though they could see everything.

Zoe shivered and pulled her jacket in around her, even though it was only minus ten and the sun was warm on her face.

The man looked up at her. "Hello."

He was wearing a light jacket and black runners. He would get maybe half a mile cross-country in those and even less far at night when the temperature dropped. What was he thinking?

"Hi," Zoe replied. "Did you hit a deer?"

He shook his head. "I came to see you. May I come up and speak to you?"

Zoe's heart pattered a little faster. "I don't know you."

"I know. I'm quite harmless," he said. "I've come a long way, too."

Her instincts were against the idea of talking to him. She hesitated.

He was looking at the peaks behind the house. "Is there a way to get to Revelstoke that doesn't use the bridge?" he asked.

"Sure. There's a trail that goes over the shoulder of the mountain and into town, only it's impassable at this time of year."

"No other way?"

"Not unless you can fly. We just use the truck."

He glanced back down the long drive toward the tree line and the bridge. "That's what I was afraid of," he said quietly, almost to himself. He climbed the steps up to the verandah and came toward her. "I'm going to have to dump this on you. We don't have time."

"Dump what?"

Up close, Zoe could see his unshaved chin, dark with growth, and his even darker eyes. He had moved in a way that spoke of reined-in and controlled strength, well beyond the capabilities of a man of his build.

She had seen that sort of control before. Startled, she studied him anew, looking for more signs. The stubble was not right. It was a human thing.

His eyes narrowed. "Perhaps I don't have to dump as much as I thought," he said quietly.

Zoe drew in a deep breath and glanced at the front door, which was still half open. "You'd better come inside," she said. "Keep your voice down. I don't want you to wake my husband."

His brow lifted. "There's just the two of you here?" he asked sharply.

"We're only five miles from town. It's not *that* isolated here."

His jaw rippled, as if he could say more yet chose not to. "Inside would be better," he said, instead.

Zoe led him inside and shut the door. She shucked off her coat and boots and took him back into the kitchen. The coffee would be nearly ready. "Coffee?" she asked him, testing.

"Thanks. I just had one," he replied.

She waved toward the kitchen table and pulled out the stool at the end of the counter and rested her hips on it, so her feet were on the floor.

He considered her again. "I said I was harmless."

"Why do you say that?"

"You have your feet on the floor, on a chair high enough that you can stand quickly. You put yourself right next to the knife block there, where all the blades are."

Her breath caught. "*What* are you?" she demanded.

"I think you know," he said quietly and scratched at his chin, "despite this."

Zoe swallowed. "Vampire…." she breathed.

"You're a hunter, which will save me hours of conversation, which we don't have time for."

"Ex-hunter. Why don't we have time?"

"How long have you been out of the game?" he asked sharply, as if it was important.

"Years. Since I left the States."

"That would explain why you didn't notice the build-up on your doorstep." He nodded toward the big windows. "You're surrounded. There are creatures out there who have no intention of letting you leave this place. When it's dark, they will come for you."

Zoe's breath squeezed out of her. "You're joking," she said. Yet she knew in her bones he wasn't. Now he had spoken of it, she could feel the darkness out there, all around the house except for where the mountain barrier sat behind them.

"Joking about what?" Cole said from the door and rubbed his hand through his tousled blond hair. He was wearing pajama bottoms and nothing else. Zoe was only thankful he'd stopped long enough to put pants on.

* * * * *

Cole stared at the Latino man, wondering if he was still dreaming. The words coming out of the man's mouth were comprehensible yet the meaning was too ridiculous to consider seriously. As the man kept talking, Cole got impatient. He put the coffee mug down with a thump.

"Diego," he said. "That's what you said your name was,

right?"

"Diego Savage," the man said. "I know this all sounds fantastic. You'll find out very quickly that I'm not exaggerating. I'm not lying at all. This really is going to happen to you." He glanced out the window again. "I hope sooner, rather than later."

"This bonding thing you keep talking about?" Cole asked. "We're supposed to be fighters in some supernatural army?"

"Cole…" Zoe said softly. She was warning him in her gentle way to keep a civil tongue in his head.

He sighed and tried again. "I don't believe in monsters, Mr. Savage."

"Cole," Zoe said, more sharply.

He looked up at her. She was standing at the corner of the counter and she was tense. "I believe him," she said quietly.

Cole laughed. "You don't even like horror movies!"

"I don't," she said calmly, "because I think they're silly, not because I don't believe in monsters."

Cole stared at her, trying to get his mind around the fact that his wife, who was the calmest and sanest person he had ever met, was professing to believe all this mystical nonsense.

"Diego," she said softly. "Perhaps, just once, would you mind showing your fangs?"

Diego hung his head for a moment. "In the name of saving time, sure." He lifted his top lip in a snarl.

Cole stared as two long, pointed teeth descended from the gum line above Diego's normal teeth. He *watched* them descend. They weren't a prosthetic, or fake things worn over the other teeth. They *grew*, right as he watched them.

He swallowed.

The fangs withdrew as smoothly as they had extended and Diego stopped snarling.

"Vampires don't like to show their fangs," Zoe said. "For them, it's a bit like being naked, all mixed up with sex and procreation."

Cole stared at her, amazed that Zoe was speaking these words with the same calm gentleness she used to speak of grocery lists and canning produce for the cold cellar. "How do you know that?" he asked, the question only occurring to him after his amazement faded.

"Remember I told you I was a bounty hunter when I lived in the States?" she asked.

He nodded. "Yeah. Bail enforcement agent. You worked with bail bondsmen in California."

She shook her head. "I was a hunter, only I didn't hunt human fugitives."

Cole turned to look at the man, the thing, called Diego. It shook its head. "Vampires haven't been on the hunting lists for centuries," Diego said shortly. "We're hunters ourselves, now. It suits our natural talents."

"You're…a monster," Cole said slowly.

"The *real* monsters are out there," Diego said, nodding toward the windows. "Which is why I need you to move past all your shock and indignation about your wife hiding her real past. Accept that vampires are real. So are lots of other things that go bump in the night and the really nasty ones are all around your house, waiting for nightfall."

Cole gripped his coffee mug. "So I could gut you with my hunting knife and you'd live anyway?"

"I'd get pissed and I would bleed all over your kitchen and it would waste another few minutes. You have to focus, Cole."

He blinked. "How am I supposed to believe you?"

"Drive down to the bridge. Try to drive over it," Diego said. "Only, take a gun with you."

"I don't have a gun," Cole said. "What's out there?"

"Go and see," Diego said impatiently. "Go on. I'll wait. Just…be careful. Don't get too close. They ripped the sides out of my car."

Cole stared at him, weighing it up. He settled, as he usually did, on the side of action first. He got to his feet.

"Cole, no," Zoe protested, jumping to her feet. "You don't know what they're like. They'll kill you."

"I have to see for myself," he said.

Zoe followed him to the front door. Her face was pale.

"You don't understand this world," she said softly. "They're more than your average bear."

He pulled on his coat and zipped it up over his bare chest and shoved his feet into the open tops of his boots. He didn't bother with the laces. He wouldn't be going far.

He dug the truck keys out of the pocket of his coat and touched Zoe's cheek. "It'll be fine," he told her.

As he opened the door, righteousness filled him. This was the smart move. This would dispense with all the nonsense inside five minutes, then he could toss the idiot, talk Zoe back to sense and get on with his day. He had a report to write about the campers they'd hauled to the medical center last night. Minor frost bite—they were lucky. It was only minus ten. By January it could drop to forty below at night around here and frost bite would be the least of their concerns.

His mind already turning over the phrases he would need for the report and the information he would pass along to his captain that *wouldn't* be in the report, Cole bounced down the steps and over to his truck.

He came to a halt, the keys swinging on the end of his fingers, as he saw the battered Mustang next to it.

Zoe and the man, Diego, were both on the verandah watching him. Zoe had pushed her feet into her boots, but wasn't wearing a coat. She had her arms crossed over her chest for warmth.

Cole gripped the keys to stop them swinging. Slowly, deliberately, he walked around the Mustang. His circuit complete, he examined the caved-in side and the ruined paintwork.

His heart started working as if he was climbing the knees of mountains, only he was just standing there. He looked up, toward the bridge. He had seen that view thousands of times.

There were shadows among the edges of the trees that weren't normally there.

Cole recognized the sour ache in his chest and the high singing in his mind. He remembered it from combat. The pre-action adrenaline rush. His gut was getting him ready while his mind was still trying to encompass that fighting was on the cards at all.

Slowly, he climbed back up onto the verandah.

Zoe lowered her arms, puzzled. "Cole…?"

"Back into the house," he said, his voice low. "Both of you."

Diego moved immediately. He understood.

Zoe frowned. "I don't get it." It wasn't often her small face wore that expression.

Cole took her arm. "Come on," he said, trying to make it sound gentle. "I need food and another gallon of coffee."

She bit her lip and let him draw her into the house.

He locked the front door behind him. He had a feeling

the lock would be useless. Anything that could do that to a car would simply throw itself against the windows and roll right in like a grenade, full of whatever fury had made it decide that Cole's place was a good one to stake out.

All three of them returned to the kitchen silently and sat back down, except Zoe. She leaned her hip against the counter, one foot crossed over the other, her arms crossed. He recognized the defensive posture.

Diego was looking at him. "The marks, right?" he said.

"I've done my share of hunting," Cole said. "A deer or even a small moose could do that sort of damage to your car, only they don't have claws. There were claw marks all along both sides of the car…and they weren't bear claws. I've seen claw marks left by bears and these were too close together. The largest cat in British Columbia is the cougar and they're rare these days. Cougar claws wouldn't have dug in like that. The paneling on the car was peeled back as if it was orange skin."

Diego nodded. "They're not natural creatures."

"No," Cole agreed. "I get that." He looked at Zoe. "I really do need more coffee," he said. "Do you mind?"

She shook her head and plucked the kettle from the range and turned to the sink. In the bright sunlight pouring in the window, her short red hair glowed and Cole's heart shifted and warmth touched him, as it always did when he realized she was here in his life.

Then he looked at Diego. The man—the vampire, Cole reminded himself—was watching him closely.

"Start again," he told Diego. "This time, I'll listen."

Chapter Three

Zoe thought Diego might be happy to talk forever, especially as Cole just sat still, not interrupting, absorbing everything. There was a tiny furrow between Cole's brows which said he was concentrating. It wasn't the wholesale frown that said something had offended his sense of rightness and he was no longer listening. That deep frown had been there until he had seen the car.

It was exactly like Cole to do this. He made up his own mind. The claw marks on the Mustang had been the solid evidence he'd needed to accept everything else. Now he was just taking it on board. Processing it.

She moved quietly around the kitchen, pulling together Cole's favorite breakfast of pancakes and sausages, grilled tomato and toast while Diego continued to talk about the Grimoré, the vampeen, the hound-like creatures who had blockaded them inside their own house, pixies, demons and elves.

The war the vampires had been spearheading for nearly three years now was news to Zoe, while the idea of demons and pixies was not. She had never seen a pixie, although she had known hunters who said they had.

It was easier for her to keep moving while she listened. It hid her nervousness and let her work it off. Eventually, she put the plate in front of Cole and glanced at Diego. "You don't mind?"

"Why should he mind?" Cole asked. His tone was curious, rather than peremptory.

"Some vampires are uneasy, watching humans eat," Diego replied. "I live with a human and an elf, who both eat. It doesn't bother me at all."

Cole glanced at Zoe. She mentally sighed. They were going to have to have a long talk, later. She had explaining of her own to do.

"The human and the elf…they are your trinity?" she asked Diego.

Diego smiled and it was a startling expression, for it was soft and warm. Even the expression in his eyes gentled. "I sometimes forget that's why we met, but yes. We were the third trinity to form."

Cole paused, the first forkful of pancake not quite reaching his mouth.

Diego gave a self-conscious laugh and used both hands to ruffle his shaggy hair and push it back out of the way. "It would be better if Seaveth was here to explain things. She makes it sound like a better proposition than I can. She sees the big picture. Me, I just look for the next vampeen I can kill."

Cole swallowed. Then he ate the pancake, concentrating on it.

Zoe bit her lip. Diego didn't like talking about slippery emotions any more than Cole did, apparently. Yet the rich feeling that had shown on his face just then, when he had thought of his two...his trinity, had been more convincing than a thousand words, or the big picture that Seaveth might have offered.

"There's one thing that doesn't make sense," Cole said. "You keep talking about trios and threes and trinities, as if it's the magic number. Only, there are two of us in the house. That's it. Why are these...vampeen...why are they surrounding the house if there's just two? The trinity can't form until the third is here. That's what you said, right?"

It was Diego's turn to frown.

The sound of a cell phone ringing was unexpected and Zoe jumped. It wasn't her phone or Cole's.

Diego dug into his jacket and pulled out a phone and glanced at the screen. "It's Seaveth," he said, glanced at them both. "I have to take this." He got up and strode out of the kitchen into the front hall, the phone to his ear. "Beth, hi...yeah, I know....yeah, British Columbia...."

Cole stopped eating as soon as Diego disappeared. He looked at her. His hazel eyes were steady.

"It's not you I lied to specifically," she said. "Hunters

don't talk about their lives to anyone. I'm one of the rare ones who managed to get out of the business and live a normal life. I thought I had left all of it behind in the States."

Cole considered her. "I can understand not talking about it," he said slowly. "But Zoe, not even to me?"

She pressed her fingers together. Twined them. "I wanted to be normal. I just wanted to be your wife and have a normal life. I thought that, if I told you, you….." She couldn't make herself say it.

"You thought I wouldn't love you anymore." He said it calmly.

Zoe nodded. Her heart was throwing itself against her chest. Hurting. Cole was studying her in the deliberate way he had.

"You're not the person I thought I loved," he said, his voice low.

Tears burned in her eyes and she blinked. "I am that same person," she said, her voice hoarse. "There's just more to me than you realized, that's all."

Cole sat back, the chair creaking with his weight. He was still shirtless and his tanned flesh was smooth and as Zoe knew personally, soft to the touch. The muscles beneath were not, however. He was a physical man and the width of his shoulders and back and the trim waist showed that. It made her a little crazy to look at him in the low-slung pajama pants, even while they were talking about such horrible things.

He was stroking his thumb over a crease in his pajamas, concentrating on it. "I guess…we both have pasts, don't we? I thought it was just me with all the baggage and you managed to encompass *my* history. Maybe I need to do the same thing with you."

Hope stirred. Zoe stayed silent, waiting, as Cole sorted it out.

* * * * *

As he clutched the phone and listened, Diego rubbed at the back of his neck, digging the fingers in. It wasn't tight back there, yet stress could make a vampire *think* their muscles were tightening up, ghostly reminders of when they had been human.

"There's a reason the trinity formed where it did," Beth said, her voice choppy. She was somewhere in Illinois, her call relayed back to the New York office, where Zack and Lindal were, then on to Diego. People were patching in every few seconds, as Lindal sent out the number. All of them were trinity people, so Diego wasn't self-conscious about it. He knew and trusted every single one of them, now he had gone through his own bonding and understood how powerful it was.

"The trinity formed in Erie because there were thousands of vampeen building in the forests there," Beth continued. "This second wave of trinities seem to form where they're most needed. From what you are saying, Diego, it appears your trinity is needed in northern Canada."

"Except it's not a trinity," he said flatly. "That's what I don't get. The vampeen are here. Their hounds are here. There's probably a bunch of Grimoré handing out orders somewhere nearby, too. There always is. With this many, I would have said they were targeting the town. Revelstoke."

"Except they're not," Blake said. "They're focusing on a house outside town that doesn't have a complete, unbonded trinity in it. There are two and they're already bonded in the human way. I don't understand it either."

"The force that drives the bondings always knows what it is doing," Beth said serenely.

"Hounds," someone who sounded a lot like Alexander said. "What next? Vampeen cats?"

"They wouldn't use cats," another voice said.

From the flat serious tone, Diego thought it might be the demon from the Pennsylvania trinity. *Demon.* Aithan corrected Diego every time he said the word. Incubi were demi-demons in Diego's mind. He had killed more than his share of the bastards. Yet Aithan *was* different. In the inner recesses of his mind, Diego acknowledged that Aithan seemed, well, almost human. Except he seemed to have lost his sense of humor somewhere in the last few centuries.

"Cats do not know how to obey their masters," Aithan

added now. "Dogs are pack animals, bred to obey their alpha and would be useful to the vampeen."

There was a small silence as everyone adjusted to Aithan's straight answer in response to Alexander's joke.

That was when the photo jumped off the mantelshelf.

The fireplace was a huge, raw stone thing, typical of log cabins and scaled to match the size of the room. The stone mantelshelf was built into the rock wall that climbed all the way to the ceiling, twelve feet above. The center of the ceiling was even higher, where the roof peaked. More massive tree trunks were running across the space as exposed trusses. The window at the end of the room was a huge three piece aperture, the triangle-shaped pane at the top matching the slope of the roof. The view beyond of snow-covered mountains and wide blue sky made the window a perfect frame.

The room was warm, comfortable and overstuffed and included dozens of pictures in frames sitting on the mantelshelf along with knickknacks, trophies and more. It was incredibly homey and the sense of permanence and belonging were not lost on Diego. He'd just been too busy with the phone call and sorting out who was talking to let it register more than skin deep.

Places like this had once made him uneasy, filling him with an almost violent resentment that such permanence and sense of family could never be his. Now, though, he had

Blake and Sera and that made all the difference in the world.

He lowered the phone, looking at the picture laying face-down on the rug in front of the unlit fireplace.

There were no air currents in the room. There was nothing that could possibly make a picture leap off a perfectly stable shelf like that.

Even with the phone lowered, he could hear Wyatt talking about gatherings and concentrations, his voice emerging from the phone in wisps. Wyatt was a damn good hunter and tended to think in hunting terms even when dealing with the Grimoré. Diego stopped listening. There were more than enough experts on everything listening in on the call.

Instead, he went over to the photo and picked it up. He flipped it over in his hand and looked at it.

Understanding flared in him. He lifted the phone back up to his face. "Gotta go."

He hung up, cutting the squawks and demands for explanations off short.

Diego—the vampire, Cole deliberately reminded himself—walked back into the kitchen. It was getting easier to think and speak the word without wanting to laugh at himself. The claw marks on the car were indisputable. He kept coming back to that over and over. *Something* had battered the car almost to pieces and it wasn't a bear or a cat. Every time the conversation became too surreal, he reminded himself of the car.

Diego laid one of their family pictures in the middle of the round table and left his finger resting on one of the faces. "Who is this?" he demanded.

Zoe grew very still. She could see the photo from where she was standing at the counter.

Cole lifted himself up off the chair just high enough to see which photo Diego had laid there.

Something crimped his gut. He took a breath, easing it. "That's…that *was* Declan."

The photo was one of the rare ones of him and Declan together. It occurred to him that it had been Zoe who had taken the photo. She was one of the very small handful of people who had known both of them.

Diego nodded. "He's dead, isn't he?"

Zoe drew in a sharp breath.

Cole swallowed. "Yes," he said flatly. It was easier to say the word using the same emotionless tone Diego had used.

Diego shook his head. "That's why there are only two of you." He said it to himself, sounding almost amused. "I never thought that…." He looked at Zoe. "Do you have any candles? A white one?"

She blinked. "I have some emergency candles in the sink cabinet."

"Could I have one? Matches, too." He picked up the photo and spread the stand behind it so the frame stood on the table.

"What are you doing?"

"I'm not a medium, although I've seen it done and I know the Latin," Diego said. He pointed at the nearly empty plate in front of Cole. "Are you done? Thanks." He picked up the plate and the cutlery and dumped them on the counter. Then the coffee cup, clearing the table of everything but the photo.

Zoe held out the candle and a book of matches silently. She didn't look puzzled.

"Latin?" Cole repeated.

"A summoning spell," Zoe told him.

"To summon what?" Cole asked. It was suddenly hard to breathe. Even his heart seemed to grow still while he waited for the answer, because part of him already knew what the answer would be.

"To summon spirits," Zoe said.

Diego shook his head. "If I'm right, we're dealing with way more than a simple spirit." He lit the candle, let it burn for a few seconds, then dropped some wax onto the table in front of the photo. He mired the end of the candle in the hot wax and held it until it was standing securely on its own. "Hush for a bit," he said, holding both hands around the flame.

Then he removed his hands and let them hang by his sides and began to speak in a slow, deep voice. *"Spiritus esto animo ostendunt, spiritum vere venistis ad me, ut sciam quod!...Spiritum esto animo ostendunt, spiritum vere venistis ad me, ut sciam quod...Spiritus ...."*

The chanting went on. Diego didn't move, apart from his mouth. He stared into the candle flame and spoke the gibberish with a slow, patient voice.

Cole looked around the kitchen, battling conflicting emotions. It was ten in the morning on a cold October day, with the sun shining in the windows. The old clock was ticking on the wall. He could still taste a perfectly normal breakfast in his mouth and the coffee that only Zoe seemed to make properly. His always tasted like sludge, even freshly made.

On the other hand, this man, this vampire, was speaking Latin to bring forth a spirit. To bring Declan back.

Cole had managed to nominally accept everything Diego had told him so far. This, though...this was impossible. It would end up being the joke that brought the whole house of lies tumbling down.

"Hey." Declan's voice, sounding mildly surprised.

Zoe gasped, holding back the squeaky sound with both hands, her eyes huge.

Cole turned on his chair, his heart trying to ram itself out of his chest. He gripped the back of the chair.

Declan stood by the counter, just as he had a thousand times before. He was wearing faded jeans and the pale blue tee shirt he had professed was his favorite and wore whenever he could.

Cole let out a breath that was more of a groan. He was shaking.

Declan was frowning, looking around the room. "I was only gone a minute, yet it's different...."

Diego picked up the candle and blew it out. He pulled out his phone, thumbed a speed dial number and listened, while watching Declan.

Cole didn't dare move. He was afraid that if he did, this moment would shatter and be gone. He could *see* Declan. He looked whole and very much alive. Even his chin was dark with stubble as it nearly always had been. His black hair was falling over his forehead, the thick waves unruly and uncontrollable.

"Hey, yeah..." Diego said into the phone. "So there is a third here, after all." He listened for a moment. "No, not a vampire," he said. "Try this on for size. It's a ghost."

Chapter Four

Declan stared at the one stranger in the room. "Ghost?" he repeated.

Zoe and Cole were both looking at him, their eyes large. Zoe was white. Cole looked as though he was going to collapse…or leap on him. His knuckles on the back of the chair were as white as Zoe's face.

"I'm the ghost…." Declan breathed as the truth gelled. He looked down at his hands, turning them over and over. "I don't feel any different."

The swarthy stranger nodded. "You feel exactly as you felt when you died. Normal. Human. Only, you're not."

"I *buried* you," Cole breathed, his voice thick with pain. He glanced at Zoe. "We buried you."

Zoe hadn't moved. A single tear rolled down her cheek. "We can see you. We can talk. We just can't touch you," she whispered.

Declan shook his head. "I *can* feel. Look." He slapped his hand on the counter…and his hand moved right through it. He could feel pressure and heat as it passed through, but nothing stopped his hand from falling back to his side. He did it again, then lifted his hand to look at it. It looked the same. There was even the little scar by his thumb, where Cole had slipped with the big screwdriver when they had swapped out the engine in his Chevy....

Cole was still staring at him, his lips parted and his eyes narrowed with pain. His throat was working.

Declan looked at the stranger, who seemed to know what was going on. "Why did you do this? Why tease him this way?"

The stranger shook his head. "This isn't some cruel trick designed to torment anyone. You're needed, Declan. You are the last of this trinity and the bond will make you all stronger...strong enough to face the Grimoré and help us win back the world."

Declan stared at him, trying to put it together. "What?"

The man grinned, his features lightening. "I get that re-action a lot. Zoe and Cole can explain it all to you." He looked at them. "Normally, we'd get the hell out of your life and let you bond in private. I think I'd better stick around, though. I'm going to stay in the hall and keep an eye on the bridge. You really don't have a gun in the house?"

Cole didn't move.

Zoe shook her head. "Nothing like that."

The man sighed and slid the largest knife out of the knife block on the counter. The block was new. That was something Cole had always wanted. The man hefted the knife as if he knew what he was doing with it.

"Take your time," he said, talking to all three of them. "Only, don't take *too* long, if you can help it."

Declan watched him leave, then looked back at the table. "Cole?"

Cole blinked. "I'm getting a headache," he breathed and gripped his head with one big hand.

"More coffee," Zoe said firmly. "And chocolate chip cookies."

"Sugar, yes," Cole said. He dropped his hand and looked at Declan. "You'd better sit down. Can you? Sit down, I mean?"

"I don't know," Declan said truthfully. He took a step toward the table. His legs worked normally. The floor felt solid beneath him as it always had. He took another step. "I'm really dead?"

"You don't remember dying?" Cole asked.

"What happened?"

"There was an avalanche on Mt. Revelstoke. The main ski slope. You were helping a man with a busted leg...." Cole stopped, his throat working. His eyes were glittering.

"The man with the broken leg was dug out," Zoe said from behind Declan, where she was working on the stove. "They couldn't get to you in time." Her voice was even. Almost serene.

Declan stopped by the chair the other man had been

using. It was still pulled out from the table. He wasn't willing to try touching it.

Cole's shoulders were shaking, his head down.

Zoe walked right around the counter, a big loop over to Cole. She put her arms around him and he turned his face into her torso and closed his eyes.

Declan stared at them. "You're...together," he breathed. He looked at Zoe's hand, at the ring there. Pain slammed into his chest. "You're *married*."

Zoe's face was pinched, tight with hurt. "You died four years ago, Declan."

He couldn't pull it together. It was a confused mess. He could almost remember the ski hill, the exhausting slog up the slope to where the skier had been laying. Only, the memory wouldn't form into an image. The cold, though.... "I remember the cold." It had been all around him, pressing in. He took a deep, sharp breath. Then let it out. "I'm breathing," he said.

Zoe shook her head. "You just think you are. You're an image, a representation of your spirit, that's all, Declan." She spoke firmly, as someone who was confident they knew what they were talking about. Declan remembered using that tone with his patients.

He pursed his lips together and whistled, the same off-key sound he had only ever been able to make. "Could I do that, if I'm just an illusion?"

Cole looked at him. Zoe let Cole go, also staring at Declan. "The bonding…." she said slowly. "Diego said it would change us."

"*And* you're sitting," Cole said slowly. He ground the heels of his hands against his eyes and gave a big, gusty sigh.

Declan looked down at the chair beneath him. He didn't remember sitting. Yet he could feel the chair beneath him. It was the same hard, unforgiving wooden seat he remembered. *That* hadn't changed.

He looked up at Zoe and Cole. "How long?" he asked.

They glanced at each other.

"Were you together before I died?" Declan demanded.

"No!" Zoe cried. "You two were *married*, Declan."

Cole shook his head. "It just happened. Long after you were gone."

"No, I don't think so," Declan said slowly. "You wanted her, even when I was alive. I saw you watching her."

Cole's jaw rippled. "You wanted her, too. You'd come home from the clinic in a muck sweat and drag me into the bedroom. Afterward, the conversation always seemed to come around to Zoe. I'm not stupid, Declan."

Declan froze. He couldn't hear his heart beat and didn't know if he was supposed to or not. Yet he *was* feeling… yeah, it was guilt.

Cole just looked at him, waiting for him to acknowledge the truth.

Zoe cleared her throat, a harsh, deliberate sound that still sounded feminine and light. "Well, this conversation has taken a detour."

"Has it?" Declan asked curiously. "You're in the room, Zoe. Cole always started thinking about sex when you were there."

"So did you," Cole said heavily.

Declan was watching Zoe, though. There was something driving him, making him want to reach for her. In all the years he had known Zoe, he had always been able to hold himself back despite the desire to touch her, because ultimately, he loved Cole and didn't want to hurt him in any way.

Now, though, it was almost a compulsion to go to her. "The bonding," he said. "You'd better tell me what it is, because I think it might be working."

* * * * *

Beth glanced out the window once more. It was snowing again. Even so, she still wanted to be out there more than she wanted to be in this apartment.

The three of them were at it again, snarling at each other. The problem was Murphy. He was a shifter, a werewolf, which Noemi, a vampire, and Dane, a human hunter, had considered to be an enemy their entire lives.

Murphy was actually snarling. The inhuman sound coming from his mouth made the hairs on the back of Beth's neck stand up straight and a shiver ripple down her back. If she had heard that sound out on the street at night, she would have broken into a sprint, heading for the nearest safe place.

Beth was suddenly tired of it. They had been at this for nearly twelve hours, while Beth had also been trying to handle everything happening back in the office by remote control.

She got to her feet, grabbed Murphy by the front of his sweater and hauled him around until he was looking at her. "You, shut up." She shoved him into the chair behind him.

She pointed at Noemi. "Retract your fangs. You look like a moody teenager, showing them in that way."

Noemi's fangs retracted with a snap and she blinked.

Beth looked at Dane. "I get that werewolves are the enemy. I get that you've hunted them since you were a kid. Things have changed."

"Shifters are half-demon," Noemi said sullenly.

"Quarter demon," Murphy said. "It's not as if we like it, either."

"I'm not kissing anything with demon blood," Dane said firmly. "It's just not happening."

"Because he's a werewolf, or because he's a man?" Beth said.

Dane's mouth opened.

"Listen, all of you. You think you've got the rough end of the stick here? You think this isn't happening to everyone in the supernatural world? We're *all* having our lives rearranged for us in ways we didn't ask for, that we have absolutely no control over. Zack is one of my trinity and he's a vampire. The other is Lindal and he's elvish. They were mortal enemies and they got thrown together and had to make it work. Neither of them had ever kissed a man before and outside the trinity, they wouldn't consider it. There's a trinity up in Pennsylvania that has an incubus. Those three love each other in a way that makes it almost hard to watch." She thought of Lindal and Zack as she had last seen them, sitting at opposite ends of the sofa, their feet tangling, laughing at each other as they fought for foot space. "Zack and Lindal love each other, too. I don't think either of them ever expected that to happen."

Dane and Noemi and Murphy were watching her now.

Beth smiled at them. "The bonding wrenches your life around, yet it also changes you in ways you can't anticipate. There are compensations that make it worthwhile. No, more than that. You'll end up wondering how you lived without each other."

"You're talking about love," Dane said quietly.

"Of *course* I'm talking about love," Beth said hotly. "If you three just give the bonding a chance to make itself felt, you'll understand what I mean."

Something shifted in Noemi's face. A shadow.

"Don't let love scare you," Beth said, her voice softer. "It makes up for everything the bonding asks of you."

"*This* is how we will defeat the Grimoré?" Dane asked.

Beth sighed. "With love? No. Love will make us stronger, though." She looked around at all three of them. "Okay? Can I leave you alone now?"

It took a moment. Finally, all three of them nodded. They were looking at each other speculatively.

Beth sighed and thought of the office in New York and jumped there.

Zack looked up from the computer he was working on as she landed. "Still trying to kill each other?" he asked.

"I think a truce has been reached," she said tiredly.

"What cudgel did you use to get that?"

Beth grinned. "I told them about you two enemies playing footsies."

Zack rolled his eyes. "He's still a bastard Son of Morning, even if he does make good food."

"I heard that," Lindal said from behind her. His lips pressed against her neck. "Green tea and a sandwich," he added.

"Oh, I *love* you," Beth said and turned to face him. The tea was sitting on her desk, steaming gently. Lindal held out the plate with the sandwich.

"I'm on with Aithan and Rhys and Cora," Zack said.

She took the plate and suppressed her sigh. "On speaker?"

"Hi, Seaveth," Cora said, her voice clear over the speaker. "I bet my bread is better than Lindal's, though."

"No contest," Lindal said quickly. "The smell of yeast upsets me for a week."

"Is there a problem, Cora?" Beth asked. Lindal led her firmly to her chair and pushed her into it and put the sandwich in front of her.

"Rhys is talking about resigning as sheriff," Zack said.

"Rhys?" Beth asked.

"Here," Rhys said, his voice strained. "I don't know how much longer I can go on with this double life. Cora has given up her day job and spends all her time, day and night, hunting the bastards down. Aithan didn't have a human life to give up in the first place. I spend my nights hunting vampeen then have to spend all day being sheriff. I can't do both equal justice and sheriff is not exactly a job you can sleep on."

"I realize it's hard," Beth said. "I really need you in that authority position, Rhys. You can do so much more there to help protect humans than we can do just hunting down vampeen when we find them. You can affect real change."

"I've already put a nighttime curfew in place," Rhys said.

"There, that's exactly what I mean," Beth said. "It's not something we could have done without you." She thought quickly. "One of the trinities has a New York police lieutenant, Blake. Would it help if you talked to him? He's got a handle on how to juggle it all, although it took him a while."

"That would help, yes," Rhys said, with obvious relief in his voice.

"I'll get back to you with details. Cora, would you mind bringing Rhys to New York when I have that arranged?"

"Of course not," Cora said quickly.

"Good. Now, I must eat. I've been nursemaiding a werewolf, a vampire and a hunter, all three of them more stubborn than Zach. I'm starving."

Cora laughed, even as Zack snorted. Beth heard the phone line click and fall dead.

"Tell me about Diego's three," she said to Zack.

"Not until you take at least one bite of the sandwich," Zack said.

She took the bite, then crammed another into her mouth. She really *was* starving.

"Blake and Rhys aren't the only ones who have to learn how to juggle," Lindal said from his big chair in the corner. He refused to sit at a desk. He said it barricaded him in.

Beth waved him away and looked at Zack, chewing hard.

"They found the third," Zack said and she could tell from the little tug on the corner of his mouth that he was holding back something.

She waited him out.

"It's a ghost."

Beth stared at him. "Is that even possible? How do they seal the bond?"

"No vampire, either," Lindal said. "Every trinity so far has had at least one vampire. It's as if your lot are holding the baseline together," he said to Zack.

Zack threw a paper clip at him. "The vampires are *how* the bond is sealed." He looked back at Beth. "The ghost is an aberration. Only, we thought Aithan was an aberration until Murphy came along."

"So this might be all part of the major plan," Lindal said.

Beth nodded and swallowed. "We wait," she said firmly. "The whatever-it-is seems to know what it is doing. We have to trust it and wait."

"You know, you're going to have to come up with a better name for the whatever-it-is," Zack said.

"Why is it up to me?" Beth demanded.

"You're our great and wonderful leader," Zack reminded her.

"Who has mayonnaise on her chin," Lindal added.

Chapter Five

Zoe only sat at the table between the two of them because Cole insisted. She could barely stay in her chair. She had sat between them in this way many times in the past. Only, in those times she had not been Cole's wife. Declan had not died and she still believed she'd put the hunting world behind her for good.

It was a reminder of far more simpler times, even though in those times she had sometimes gone home with her body in a stew of unrelieved wanting. Declan's dark Irish good looks and Cole's blond, macho perfection had equal effects upon her. She had never tried to sort out in her mind which of them she wanted more because ever having either of them was completely out of the question.

Except now, if she understood Diego properly, she could have *both* of them.

It was all she could think about. It was throbbing in her mind, making her body pulse and her nerves sizzle. She was far more wound up than she had ever been when Cole and Declan had been married...

Her breath squeezed out of her. Cole and Declan had

been married. She was the interloper.

She looked from one to the other of them, dismay building. Declan had been Cole's great love and his death had just about destroyed him. She had always known Cole had reached for her to prop himself up. It hadn't mattered. She was one of the few people who had known the two were even lovers, let alone married, so she had understood Cole's grief.

The depth of her own grief had shocked her. She hadn't been aware of how deeply Declan had worked his way into her heart, until he had died.

Now he was sitting next to her once more, looking exactly as he had always looked. Slightly scruffy, sinfully sexy, his eyes hooded and brooding as he considered Cole, who had finally finished explaining about the Grimoré, the vampire-led defense against them and the trinities.

Declan turned his gaze upon Zoe. "You're a hunter, then? I mean, you know this world? You knew it before."

She nodded. "I thought I'd left it behind," she added.

"It's a long way from being my medical assistant," he agreed.

"That was the point. It was the complete polar opposite."

"You killed things."

"Evil things," she replied.

"So, with this bonding, that is what I will become? A

fighter in this war?"

Zoe's heart squeezed. "I suppose...yes," she said carefully.

Declan looked at Cole. "You're the professional soldier. Zoe, too, I guess. I'm not a fighter, Cole. Not even now. I will not kill another...not even a creature that isn't human."

Cole shook his head. "You haven't seen them."

"Neither have you!" Declan declared. "I'm a doctor! I *heal* people. It's all I've ever wanted to do and now you're telling me some supernatural force that even the vampires don't understand properly has decided I must pick up a knife or a gun and kill these things I have never seen?"

Zoe realized her hand had lifted toward him. She had been reaching for him. Only, she couldn't do that. Neither could Cole. Neither of them could touch him or comfort him.

Yet her whole body yearned to do exactly that.

She put her hand back in her lap. "None of us knows how this will work out," she said. "Every trinity is different in some way."

Declan blew out his breath and shoved his hands through his hair. The same thick lock curved over his forehead once more. "If I have to fight, then I don't want to be here," he said flatly, looking at Cole.

Cole just looked at him. "Okay," he said at last. "I don't think I could bear to see you fighting, either. If it comes to that, we'll figure it out. Only, for right now, just for a moment, can we…can I enjoy just being able to talk to you again?"

"I mean it, Cole," Declan said heavily. "I'll do whatever ghosts do when they want to be gone. I *will not fight*."

"I hear you," Cole said quietly. Firmly.

It was the same iron-cored tone he always used when he meant what he said. Cole never promised, yet if he said he'd take care of something in that tone of voice, Zoe had learned he would move mountains to make it happen. He was a man of his word.

She looked from one to the other of them, her heart thudding. It wasn't the low-grade arousal this time. It was unhappy recognition. They had forgotten she was in the room. It was just the two of them, communing on a level forever barred to her because they didn't love her the way they loved each other.

Now Declan was back, even in this limited way, could she really insert herself between them the way Diego was implying would happen?

Before she realized she had even made the decision, she was on her feet and moving through to the hallway and the front door.

"Zoe!" Declan called, startled.

She kept going.

"Zoe, come back." Cole sounded just as surprised.

53

Diego was sitting on the bench beneath the coat rack, his back against Cole's long formal overcoat, the cell phone to his ear. He looked startled as she headed for the door.

"I'll call back," he said shortly into the phone and put it away. "Where are you going?"

"Doesn't matter," she said woodenly and dug in Cole's casual coat for the truck keys.

"You can't leave," Diego said urgently. "They won't let you. They'll tear you to pieces. You're one of the trinity and you'll be offering yourself up to them."

"Don't care," she replied and opened the front door. Her first step onto the verandah and the cold wooden planking reminded her she only wore socks and no coat. She shrugged and kept going, down the steps and across the gravel that dug into her feet with painfully sharp points.

"Zoe!" It was Declan, again.

She didn't look up from opening the truck door. The lock had frozen last winter and now it was always stiff to open and took all her strength. Cole made it look easy, as if there was nothing wrong with it. Cole....

Her eyes pricked with scalding tears.

"Zoe," Declan said and this time he was much closer.

She looked up, blinking rapidly to clear her tears.

He was standing next to the truck. Next to her. "Where do you think you're going?" he asked, his voice low and soft.

"You don't need me," she said. "Neither of you."

Cole was standing on the verandah, leaning on the railings. Even though he was half naked and barefoot he didn't seem to notice the cold. He was watching them with peculiar intensity.

Diego was standing in the doorway, watching just as intensely.

"Why are *you* talking to me?" Zoe asked Declan. "Why not Cole?"

Declan didn't look at Cole. "If Cole asks you to stay, you'll believe him, yet you will still doubt me. Only, I don't want you to leave, either. So I'm asking."

"Why?" she asked, anger stirring. She was being pulled apart here. Couldn't he see that? "You've suddenly discovered in the last sixty seconds that you love me, after all?"

"It has been much, much longer than sixty seconds." His voice was low.

Zoe stared at him. He looked back, his expression calm, his eyes the same black as always.

Over his shoulder, she saw Cole's head bend. His eyes were closed.

"Cole needs you more." Her voice was hoarse with unshed tears. She finally got the door open.

"No," Declan said swiftly. He put his hand against the door and shoved it back. It slammed closed.

Zoe gasped and stepped back, looking from the door to Declan. Her heart was thundering again. "You moved it."

Declan looked at his hand in wonder. "The bonding," he said softly. "It's really working."

Zoe swallowed.

Declan held his hand out to her, for her to take it. "Come back inside. Please."

Zoe looked at Cole once more. He was gripping the support post. When her gaze met his, he nodded. It was a tiny movement, yet it was enough for her to take Declan's hand.

His hand was cool, but so was hers, out here.

Declan looked down at her hand. "So small," he murmured.

"My wedding ring fits *through* Cole's," she said. It was something she had said dozens of times, to her co-workers at the clinic and to friends. Even she and Cole had laughed about it.

Declan didn't smile. "Mine didn't." The tug on her hand was slight, yet it was there. "Please, Zoe. Let's talk. Let's *really* talk."

She let him draw her back inside.

When Zoe reached the verandah level, she tried to slip her hand free from Declan's. His grip tightened. She could barely look at Cole, although from the corner of her eye she watched him straighten and head back inside. Even Cole could not withstand the cold for too long, despite physically challenging himself in small ways like this.

Diego, though, was standing just inside the front door. He hadn't moved and he was staring at the door sill, frowning.

"Something wrong?" Zoe asked him. She had known a few vampires in the past and had learned to rely on their instincts, which were driven by far more powerful senses than humans could aspire to.

Diego pushed the toe of his shoe up against the sill itself. "Recognize that?" he asked quietly.

She peered at the tile and grout where it met the wood sill. There was dried mud there, tracked in by snowy boots, that she had not swept up properly. Among the grit, though, was a pale yellow sand. The particles were very fine and stirred in the air moved by Diego's shoe. So, not sand. Something lighter.

"Pixie dust," Diego said, his voice still soft. He looked up and around the hallway.

"Here?" Zoe breathed. "I thought they distrusted humans."

"They hate *them* more," Diego said, nodding toward the bridge. "You can't speak their name in front of them. It freaks them out." He moved back to the bench under the coats. "They might emerge, now the bonding has started and has marked you all. Or they might not."

"You know, you could sit in the lounge room and be comfortable, if you really must stay here," she told him.

Cole and Declan had already moved back into the kitchen, although Declan hovered by the door, waiting for her.

"You might want to use the room," Diego pointed out. "I'm fine here. I have a lot to do." He sat on the bench.

"Like what?" Zoe asked, puzzled.

"Oh, hello." It was a woman's voice. A strange one.

Zoe turned, startled.

A tall woman with masses of long golden blonde hair and very large blue eyes was standing in the middle of the hallway. Zoe had a hard time pulling her gaze away from her face. Her skin seemed to glow. She wore perfectly normal jeans and a sweater.

"You're elvish," Zoe said. She could feel her cheeks burning. "I mean...I'm sorry. You're my first elf."

The woman smiled and it was a lovely expression that made Zoe feel warm and happy. "I am Seramela. You can call me Sera."

Zoe didn't offer her hand. It was only humans who used the practice of shaking hands with a stranger.

"I'm Declan," Declan said, coming up behind her.

Sera smiled at him, too. "And you are my first ghost," she said.

Declan shrugged. "I'm the first ghost I've ever met, too."

"Diego tells me you are also a healer."

Zoe glanced at Diego, startled. None of them had mentioned that to him.

Diego lifted his phone. "It's all over the Internet."

Declan's smile was warmer. "I was a doctor," he agreed.

"You still are," Sera said firmly. "The urge to heal does not fade."

As Declan studied her, surprised, she turned to Diego and lifted a tangle of leather and buckles and two holsters, both with pistols in them. "Your spares, as requested."

Diego got to his feet and kissed her and it was not a polite peck. "You are ever my savior."

She laughed and dropped the bag in her left hand to his feet. "More supplies, including the machete." She looked around the hall. "What a beautiful house," she added. Then she smiled up at the ceiling. "Well, hello there."

Zoe looked up quickly. There was nothing there.

"On the top beam," Sera said softly. "They're very shy. They seem to like elves, though. Lindal has a friend who almost lives on his shoulder."

"Ferr," Zoe said. "Diego told us about her."

Sera looked around the hall once more, taking in everyone there, including Cole, who was standing in the kitchen doorway now, his chest still bare. "I'm interrupting," Sera said. "I also left behind three vampires who are dealing with their own bonding, who I should get back to."

Diego tilted his head. "They're still fighting it?"

Sera looked troubled. "They have all been passing as human. One has a fiancé. It is…difficult."

"The bonding will change that," Diego said. "I was more stubborn than most and it worked on me."

Sera looked at Zoe and rolled her eyes. "He caved, the moment he saw me."

Zoe fought not to laugh as Diego looked affronted.

Sera spread her hands. "I really must not linger. Call if you need me." She held her hand out to Diego and he caught the tips of her fingers with his, then let her go. It was a barely there touch, yet their expressions made Zoe feel embarrassed she was witnessing the highly intimate moment.

She glanced at Declan. He was watching the pair with his dark eyes narrowed, a look of heavy concentration on his face. She had seen that expression many times before, when he had been dealing with a tricky diagnosis.

Sera lifted her hand in a small wave goodbye and disappeared.

Diego stirred and returned to the bench. He did not look awkward about having been seen showing such raw emotions.

"I think I understand…." Declan breathed.

Diego looked at him. "Good," he said flatly. "Go. Go and talk." He sat down. "Have your discussion. Let the bond arrange things, while I take care of the rest." He yanked one of the pistols from the harness, pulled out the clip and checked it, then snapped it back with a practiced motion and cocked the gun and put it beside him. He turned his head to look through the glass pane beside the door, toward the bridge.

Chapter Six

When Zoe returned to the kitchen, Cole was at the sink, his arms crossed and his butt resting on the edge of the sink itself. She had reminded him more than once not to do that, as his habit of sitting on the edge of the big farmhouse sink had broken two of them, resulting in costly replacements.

She said nothing now. All the little domestic conflicts and compromises, the rituals they had developed, including her making every cup of coffee because Cole's coffee-making skills were non-existent...all that had been superseded.

Declan opened the pantry door and looked inside.

"You're hungry?" Cole said, surprised.

Declan shook his head. "I can open the door." He closed it and opened it again and grinned.

Cole gave a weak smile.

Zoe couldn't react at all.

"I wonder if I can feel heat?" Declan murmured, heading for the range.

"Shut the door!" Cole and Zoe said, together.

Declan halted, startled, looking from one to the other.

How many times had Cole said that to him over the years? Even Zoe had got into the habit of reminding him whenever she had been visiting. It was too easy for someone else to ram up against open door and hurt themselves.

Declan moved back to the pantry door and shut it silently. He let his hand linger on the door handle, then looked up. "I remember that," he said quietly.

Cole shifted his shoulders, easing them, as if they were strained. Perhaps they were. "We need to talk."

Declan put his shoulder against the pantry door and crossed his arms, matching Cole. "Agreed."

Zoe sighed.

Cole gave them an effortful smile. "Do either of you get the feeling that this bonding thing is going to ride roughshod over all our feelings and wishes and expectations?"

"I figured that out a moment ago," Declan said. "When I saw Diego and Sera out there." He shrugged. "I don't mind. Of course I don't mind. I've got life back…and I didn't even know I had lost it."

"It's not the life you used to have," Cole pointed out.

"I don't care," Declan said firmly. He pressed his hand against his chest, his fingers digging in. "I can *feel* and not just with my hands and nerves." He dropped his hand. "If I get to have even a small fraction of what Sera and Diego seem to have, then I *really* don't care about the rest." His black gaze settled on Zoe. "You're the only one fighting this, Zoe."

She was startled. She was also confused. She looked at Cole. "You're not fighting it?"

Cole drew in a breath and let it out. "Are you asking if I care that our marriage seems to have been blown apart in the last few hours, then yes, I mind…except you're still here and that's something I can work with. You scared the crap out of me when you walked out just then." His green eyes were narrowed, the way he held them when he was in pain. "Only, you came back."

"To talk," she said.

"I'm trying hard not to judge, to not use old standards." Cole grimaced. "Hell, I spent my entire adult life hiding my real nature from the whole world except for the very few people I trusted with the truth, so I know all about prejudice. I know how insidious it can be. Since I saw those claw marks on the Mustang I've been reminding myself of that over and over." He let out a breath, almost a sigh. "I think you need to let go, too, Zoe."

She jumped. "Me?"

"You're holding onto some old ways yourself," Declan said, his voice low.

Zoe pressed her lips together.

"Tell us why you walked out just then," Cole said.

"You know why." Her voice came out strained.

"I'm pretty sure I do know. Declan, too," Cole said. "I

just don't think you do."

"Of course I do!" she said hotly.

They both just looked at her.

Zoe shifted on her feet. Her socks were damp. She should take them off. Maybe get a fresh pair....

"Zoe," Declan said.

She looked at him and pushed the words out. "Cole was with you first. I can't take that away from either of you, now you've got it back."

Cole shook his head. "That's *just* like you," he said softly. "Everyone else first, while what you want is back there in the dust."

"It's called being human," Zoe said stiffly. "It's what decent people do. I grew up hunting alongside my father and that world, that life, teaches you to watch out for yourself, first and foremast. Survival is the priority. I walked away from that when my father died. I swore I would not go back to that world and here I am," she said bitterly.

"You loved your father," Declan said.

"Of course I did!"

"How did he die?" Cole asked. "I mean, the real story. He didn't die in a car accident, the way you told me, did he?"

Zoe wiped at her cheeks. "A demon took him."

"Why didn't the demon take you as well?" Declan asked.

Zoe's heart squeezed. "My father...he...." She put her

face in her hands, blocking out the light, trying to block the memory.

"He protected you," Cole guessed.

She nodded. Her throat was too tight to speak.

"So, in fact, he didn't look out for himself at all," Declan said. His voice was closer. She didn't have the courage to look. The miasmic stew of hot feelings swirling in her gut were making her feel dizzy and a little sick. "I don't want to give up this life I worked so hard to create," she said into her hands. "Only, if I fight for it, you and Cole will be hurt."

"You don't have to give up anything," Cole said, his voice gentle.

That made her look. He was calm. There was even a little smile playing around the corner of his mouth. "You said it yourself, Zoe. You said you were still the same person I always thought you were, just with additions I hadn't known were there before. That could be us, too."

"You and me?" she breathed.

He nodded. "We stay the same. We stay married, only there are additions we didn't know about before."

"Only you *did* know about Declan before!" she cried. "You *loved* him. I held you every time you cried. I listened to your stories. You bled over his loss, Cole. That gaping hole has never gone away."

Cole nodded. "We both have pasts that dog us, even now. Declan does, too. That's what makes us human. I just don't think we should go *back* there. If Diego is right, then we're all going to be something more than human. More additions."

"Additions, not subtractions," Declan added. "We include, we don't take away."

Zoe wiped her cheeks again. "That's what I'm afraid of," she said flatly. "If you include me, then you'll lose something."

Declan laughed.

Even Cole smiled. "Didn't you hear a word of what we were saying, a while ago?"

"We seem to have been talking for an ice age," Zoe said tiredly. "Remind me."

Declan answered, though. "Cole has loved you since he came back from Afghanistan the first time after he moved in here. I watched him meet you in the surgery, that day. I saw his heart drop onto the floor at your feet."

Cole was staring at the floor, a hard frown squeezing his brows together.

"You...didn't mind?" Zoe whispered to Declan. She thought her heart might explode if any more pressure was exerted.

"How could I mind?" Declan said. "I'd been in love with you for months already." He gave her a skewed smile. "Cole losing his heart just confirmed I wasn't wrong about you."

"You didn't say anything, either of you! You got married!"

Cole still wasn't looking at them. "I loved Declan more, right then. There was no way I was going to fuck that up with badly timed confessions."

Declan was nodding. "Then, you just sort of…fitted in. It was good. Life was good. I had Cole and you were still there. Not quite the way I wanted, but there anyway."

"I was so afraid that if I said *anything*, it would all explode and I would lose *everything*," Cole said. He lifted his chin and looked at Declan.

Declan nodded. "It felt so finely balanced, as if a single wrong move might destroy it all."

Zoe remembered to breathe. There were little specks dancing in her vision. "Neither of you said anything to each other? Nothing at all?"

Cole shrugged. "I knew, anyway."

"We both knew," Declan added softly. "We knew what *we* wanted, anyway. We still don't know what you want, though."

She swallowed. "As Cole said, I don't think it matters what we want anymore. The bonding is going to take care of that."

"Just this once, Zoe," Cole said. "Say what *you* want."

She rubbed her eyes. They were still aching from the tears. "I can't."

"Why not?" Declan said.

She looked at Cole. "I just can't hurt you in that way."

"You want Declan," he said flatly.

Her gut twisted. "No! I want you both! I always have!" She felt her jaw drop. So much for not hurting Cole.

Only, Cole was nodding. The small smile was back on the corner of his mouth. His eyes were warm...heated, even. He and Declan exchanged a glance that seemed to be loaded with meaning.

Declan was moving toward her, very slowly. "Do you remember that time in the surgery when we worked on that frostbite case?"

She nodded. They had used snow to keep the foot from defrosting too quickly, to restore circulation slowly so the deadened toes would be saved. She had brought bucket after bucket of snow in from the courtyard behind the surgery. "It was something I remembered from a story I'd read as a child," she said. "Except you used the idea anyway and it worked."

He nodded. "Afterward, in the staff room," he said. "Remember?"

How could she forget? They had both been reeling with the need for sleep and she had barely been able to put on her coat. Her shirt sleeve had gotten all tangled up. Declan had unsnarled it and straightened up the coat. He'd even zipped it up. For a moment his hand had stayed there just under her chin and her breath had caught.

For once, she had allowed herself to look him directly in the eye, too tired to remember she shouldn't do that.

There had been knowledge in his gaze. For that little moment, it felt as if her heart and soul was open and he was reading it all there in her eyes.

All he had to do was lift his hand a fraction of an inch and he could have touched her face. They were standing so close he could have just bent his head to kiss her.

He did neither. Instead, after that little moment had lasted for what felt like an hour or two, he stepped away. "Drive carefully," he warned her. "It's slippery out there."

She had stumbled away and driven home in a daze, wondering if she had imagined all of it. Had she projected her own yearnings onto him? Declan was happily married. Even though his marriage was a secret to almost everyone else in Revelstoke, his happiness and general air of contentedness was not. She was a fool for thinking he would consider even for a moment...

"I wanted to kiss you that night," Declan said, his voice very low. He was right in front of her now. "I don't know how I stopped myself." He glanced at Cole. Cole hadn't moved from the sink. His gaze was steady. "Well, yes, I know why I didn't. But it was very, very close."

"Kiss her now," Cole said, his voice as quiet as Declan's.

Zoe jumped a little in reaction.

"Forward, not backward," Cole added.

"Yes, that was then, with all the reasons why we should-n't," Declan added. "This is now."

Zoe gasped as his lips met hers. That he could touch her at all was a miracle. His mouth was firm against hers just as she had always imagined it might be.

Zoe closed her eyes as the kiss deepened. Her body had spent the morning being whipsawed through extremes of emotions. Now everything came on-line in a heated sweep from her toes to the top of her head.

Declan brought his arms around her, pulling her even closer and she might have cried at finally being in his arms, except that it felt so good she had no capacity for anything other than delight.

He was taller than her. Everyone was taller than her and Cole more than most, yet she fitted against Declan in a way that felt natural. She drew her arms around his neck, holding herself up as he kissed her with a thoroughness that barely made up for all the times she wished he had.

His hands were against her back, sliding over her hip, moving restlessly. Cole was strong and had muscles to prove it, while Declan was solid in a different way, firm against her body....

Zoe gasped and stepped back from him, not quite look-ing down. Her heart was frantic, her nerves screaming.

Declan, though, *did* look down at the swollen mass in

the front of his jeans. "Well, then. That answers that question." He was grinning.

"It answers mine, too," Cole said. "I thought I would mind, watching you kiss her. Yet I don't. It feels…."

"Right," Zoe finished. "As though that's the way it should be. It's as if I've kissed you hundreds of time before."

Declan nodded. "Comparison check," he declared. He took the two small steps to reach Cole and kissed him. He didn't hesitate. Their mouths pressed together and Cole rose to his feet almost as if the kiss was pulling him there. He grabbed Declan's face and held him steady.

Declan's hand settled on Cole's hip, his fingers tangling with the band of his pajama pants.

Zoe caught her breath. In her imagination, Declan did not simply let his fingers rest there. She could clearly see him in her mind, pushing the pants down farther, exposing Cole's hips, his pelvis and the ridge of muscle there, then his cock, which would be upright and throbbing.

She couldn't look away. Every erotic thought she had ever had about the pair of them, together or alone, seemed to parade through her thoughts now, making her body vibrate. They looked so good together. They always had. Declan's wild Celtic looks and Cole's blond, clean-cut wholesomeness played off each other.

Declan groaned and pulled his lips away, breathing heavily.

Cole closed his eyes, just not before Zoe saw tears glittering there. "Just the same," he said, his voice hoarse.

Her heart squeezed.

"Zoe." Cole held his hand out toward her.

She took it and he pulled her close, up against the two of them. Almost as if they had done it many times before, both of them put their arms around her, linking them all together.

They stayed there, until Zoe's heart eased. It didn't slow completely, because she was standing with the two of them. The parade of wicked images was playing in her mind, still. Now the thoughts were becoming even more erotic. Just standing here was making her think of possibilities that had not occurred to her before.

"I think," Cole said heavily, "we should go somewhere there is a door we can lock between us and the rest of the world."

"The bedroom," Zoe said, just as Declan did.

Zoe had stepped into the bedroom thousands of time before. Now, though, the room looked unfamiliar. She stopped a few feet inside the door, looking at the fireplace and the big bed and the tall windows.

This had been Cole and Declan's room, too. Only now did she remember that.

Declan's hand settled on her shoulder, making her jump. "Stop apologizing," he whispered in her ear.

"I didn't."

"In your head, you did." He moved around her. His eyes were dancing. "I think if you had walked into this room one night when we were both in it, we would have locked the door behind you and thrown away the key. You're not an intruder, Zoe. You never have been."

"She wouldn't come in here. Not for weeks," Cole said. "We would sleep on the sofa, downstairs, instead." He went into the bathroom and shut the door.

"Did you actually get any sleep?" Declan asked curiously.

Zoe could fee her cheeks heating again. "Some."

Declan's smile grew warmer. "Who kissed who first?"

"I...don't remember," she lied. They had been arguing. It had been nearly a year since Declan's funeral. Lately, all they had seemed to do was argue, getting more wound up with each passing day, although neither of them had suggested quitting the almost daily lunch dates. The argument had continued out in the restaurant parking lot as Cole strode to his truck, fishing out his keys, his hand shaking with fury. She had followed him, determined to get in the last word and she had. Then he had cut her off by spinning to face her, pulling her up against him and shutting her up with his lips.

The arguments had evaporated after that and Cole had proposed barely three months later.

Declan seemed to see the memories play in her head. "Perhaps you'll be able to tell me some other day," he said. "When you know in your heart I don't mind."

"Perhaps," she said cautiously, yet her heart had skipped a beat at the mention of future days. She had barely been able to think beyond the next moment. Days from now were blank wastelands of speculation.

The emotion in Declan's eyes grew heated. "Although if Cole took care of you the way he always took care of me, then no wonder you didn't get any sleep."

Zoe gasped softly.

Declan leaned toward her. "Between you and me," he said, his voice so low she could barely hear it. "Weren't you amazed that such a white-bread, morally upright guy could be so inventive in bed?"

Zoe could feel her eyes widen in shocked recognition. The first time they had made love had been in Cole's truck, barely minutes after that first kiss, both of them shaking with the power of their mutual orgasms. He had only put her aside long enough to put the truck in gear and drive back to the house. His jeans had stayed open, his cock beating against his stomach. His hand had wandered over her as he drove, stripping her naked there on the seat.

Then he had taken her again, parked in front of the

house and three more times between the truck and the sofa, where they had finally come to rest.

"Ay, I can see you were," Declan said. "I never could get enough of him."

Zoe dropped her gaze and Declan lifted her chin, making her look at him. "Don't," he said firmly. "It is what it is. We go on from here."

"Good advice," Cole said, as he moved toward them. "Guilt is over-rated."

"Then we're agreed," Declan said. "Now, can I kiss her again?"

Chapter Seven

It was only when Diego heard voices upstairs that he realized there was a set of stairs at the back of the house, as well
as the grand staircase here in the front hall. He listened only
long enough to confirm it was the three of them, before
shutting his hearing down by focusing on the text on his
phone and glancing out through the door pane occasionally.

Even from this far away, Diego could see the moving
shapes among the trees. They roved ceaselessly, drawing his
gaze. How long until they broke and came at the house?
Would they wait for sunset, if they realized the trinity was
sealing the bond? Even Diego could feel the building power
from the three. There was conflict there, still, mostly from
Zoe as a result of their shared history. However, Declan understood the power of the trinities. Diego hoped he would
be able to bind the three of them properly. Cole…well, he
was the unknown. He was amenable, so far, yet his whole
life had been a pattern of outwardly conforming while secretly and flagrantly rebelling against that conformity.

Something to the far left of the bridge caught Diego's
eye. He got to his feet, adjusted the sit of the gun harness

around his shoulders and peered through the left-hand side pane. There was movement there that wasn't the same as the restless circling the hounds were doing closer to the bridge.

He narrowed his eyes, bringing the details into focus.

It was a bear. The creature was sliding down the slopes of the foothills, through the trees there. Its direction would take it right into the clearing in front of the house, where the snow lay thick and untouched.

Diego pushed the door open and stepped out onto the verandah for a clearer view. Bears did not frighten him. He had the strength to tackle one if he really had to and now, thanks to Blake and Sera, he had his guns, too.

It looked as though he might not have to deal with the bear at all. It was ambling through the trees and the hounds were all heading in its direction. The hounds were big, too, and there were more of them. They might encourage the bear to go back to its den.

Den. Winter

Bears hibernate in winter.

Understanding flared in him. Diego clutched the post. "It's not a bear," he whispered, staring at the black shape as it loped through the trees.

The hounds met it with growls that rolled out over the snow. Diego's fangs descended as his animal instincts were prodded by the sound. He made them retract and waited.

The bear lifted a platter-sized paw and batted at the first hound to reach it. The hound was tossed aside, yelping in pain.

So were a third and a fourth. The bear only slowed its pace long enough to swat at each hound it passed, using its shoulders to barrel through them, much as Diego had done with the Mustang.

When the bear reached the clearing and started running through the hip-high snow, throwing up clouds of white with each loping stride, Diego pulled out one of his guns and cocked it. The bear was heading directly for the house.

The hounds stayed back at the tree line, howling and yelping.

Diego moved out to the top step and raised the gun, tracking the bear. When it reached the gravel where the snow had been ploughed away, he said, "Stop right there. These are .45s and they're silver. They might not stop a normal bear, but they'll kill you well enough."

The bear came to a halt, sniffing and breathing hard. Then it lifted up onto its back legs.

Diego watched it change calmly. He had seen shifters change before, only this time he concentrated on keeping his aim steady.

The man was older than he expected. Perhaps in his sixties, which was unusual for a shifter. They tended to die young. He was naked, of course and wrapped his arms around his middle. "I know what you are," he said. "I came to speak to you."

"Even though the vampeen control this area?"

He shrugged. "I got through. It's about the Grimoré. You're one of them, aren't you? The trinities, I mean."

Diego didn't lower the gun. "How do you know about them?"

"Everyone knows, now. Word has passed."

Diego nodded. The supernatural world had its own version of the Internet, a combination of word of mouth, telekinesis and other powers, along with ancient instincts that whispered to those who had lived long about unnamed new threats to their survival.

"Shifters are demon-blood," Diego said. "Why should I trust you?"

"You probably shouldn't. I have information you should have, though."

Diego lowered the gun. "Wait," he said. He went back in the house, grabbed the biggest coat on the rack and came back out. He tossed it onto the gravel. "Put it on. You can talk from there."

The shifter came forward and Diego could see faint scars all over his body. He had fought hard to live this long. He bent and picked up the coat and slipped it on. "Thank you."

"Talk," Diego said. He didn't aim the gun. He didn't put

it away, either.

The man's black eyes were fathomless and unreadable, just like his bear soul. "I heard there's a demon working with you."

"You said you had news."

The shifter raised his hand. It was big, just as the bear's had been. "The Grimoré are moving south. The vampeen with them. They're driving everything before them. They're eating anything they can find, too."

"You came down from the north?"

The shifter's eyes were troubled. "There are whole villages up there with not a soul left in them and no one left to report the loss." He wrapped his arms around himself again. Diego knew it wasn't for warmth this time. "Demon blood. Human blood. Elvish kind…none of us is safe anymore. Even those demons who agree to work with the Grimoré are consumed once their work is done." He smiled and his smile was bitter. "Finally, the demons are learning for themselves what it is like to make a deal with a devil."

Diego considered this. "The Grimoré are moving south?"

The shifter nodded. "I would work with you. The enemy of my enemy is my friend. I can help you defeat them. And I know others, too."

"Other shifters?"

He nodded.

"What's your name?" Diego demanded.

Something in the man's face roiled. "I was called Gilbert, once."

Diego steeled himself against the empathy that wanted to form. He remembered that sense of desolation and loneliness only too well. He put the safety on the Glock and put it away. "I'm going to have you taken somewhere safe, Gilbert. Seaveth will put you to work and you will work your paws off. Understand that no one will trust you completely, not ever, not even while you work beside them."

Gilbert sighed. "I do not blame you for that."

"If you turn on us, if your animal gets loose, I will be the first to put a bullet in your brain and I will not hesitate."

Gilbert nodded.

"If you truly want to stop these fuckers, then I welcome you to the fight," Diego told him. He pulled out his phone and dialed. "We can use all the help we can get."

Cole came right up behind Zoe and put his arms around her. He was still wearing only the pajama bottoms and his chest against her back was hot. She snuggled, closing her eyes. He often came up behind her in this way, wherever she happened to be around the house. Sometimes he would only kiss the nape of her neck. Sometimes, though, his hands would slide up to cup her breasts and tweak the nipples. Or he would strip her jeans down to her ankles, shove her panties down her legs and bend her over and slide into her, making her nerves leap to high, silvered alert.

He did none of those things now. Instead his hands settled on her hips. "It seems to me that we need an icebreaker, so Zoe can relax."

"I don't think Declan can drink," Zoe murmured. It was a miracle he could touch anything at all. Ghosts were supposed to be wisps of spirit left behind and were usually beneath a hunter's horizon of interest. "Although nothing would surprise me now."

Declan grinned. "Cole isn't talking about alcohol," he told her. His gaze met Cole's over her head. "Right?"

"Right." Cole's voice rumbled against her shoulders. "Can you take your clothes off at all? Or are you like every ghost I've ever seen in the movies, stuck the way you are?"

Declan frowned. "Good question. Let's find out." He reached for the hem of the tee shirt and lifted it. "So far, so good," he murmured. "So…." He pulled it up over his head and dropped it.

The tee shirt disappeared.

"Did I just see…did it vanish?" Cole asked.

"It was never really here," Zoe breathed. "Just as Declan isn't really here. Only his spirit is solid enough to touch, because of the bonding."

Declan looked down at his bare chest. "It's my body,"

he said.

"You've even got the same mole there, just under your pecs," Cole said.

Declan touched the little mark. "It feels normal to me. It feels just as it used to. If you two hadn't fallen apart the way you did when I arrived in the kitchen and if I didn't have a blank spot in my mind after the avalanche, I'd say you were both lying and I'm as real as you are." His hands dropped to the button of his jeans. His jeans rode low on his hips and were loose enough to slide a hand inside. Zoe suddenly itched to do just that, only she was very aware of Cole standing right behind her, his chest rubbing her back with maddening little touches, making her nerves twitch and stirring her arousal.

Instead, she fisted her hands and watched as Declan opened the button. His long, clever fingers picked up the tab of the zipper and lowered it.

"The look on your face…" he breathed.

Zoe swallowed. "I'm—"

"Don't say you're sorry," Cole said quickly. "Declan, we really need to cure her of that."

"Agreed." He pushed his jeans down his legs and stepped out of them, sliding his sneakers off at the same time. Then he straightened up, utterly naked.

Zoe caught her breath. She loved Cole's physical perfection. He had spent his years in the military and since he had left the Army, honing his body, working it hard and sculpting the muscles. Declan, on the other hand, used his intellect for his profession and although he had sometimes worked out with Cole, he wasn't nearly as interested in pushing his body and gaining every scrap of strength the way Cole was.

Even so, Declan had a well-shaped body, with plenty of muscle, just not huge amounts of it. There was absolutely no spare fat on him. His belly was flat and rippled over the muscles. His arms and shoulders were rounded and looked strong.

Zoe looked down. She couldn't help herself. Her gaze was drawn there, as if it was on rails. His cock was fully erect and beating with life. It was thick, the flared head darker on the edges.

Her heart leapt.

"You haven't changed an inch," Cole breathed. His chest was rising and falling more rapidly and she could feel *his* heart, too, beating against her.

Declan smiled. "If I'm really a ghost, then maybe I can change how I appear. Another inch might be useful."

"No," Zoe and Cole said together.

Declan looked at her. "You like what you see, then."

She cleared her throat softly. "Yes." It still came out almost hoarse.

Cole's fingers squeezed her hips. "Touch him," he said in her ear.

Her heart was slamming against her chest and her fingers felt thick and awkward as she lifted them up toward him. Her whole body felt as though it was pulsing with aching need.

It didn't surprise her to see her hand was shaking. She laid it against Declan's chest.

"You're not hot," she breathed. "Not like Cole."

"He's not cold, either," Cole said.

Declan curled his fingers around her wrist and drew her hand down, so the tips of her fingers trailed over his flesh. "Take what you *really* want," he told her and pressed her palm against his cock.

Shuddering with overwhelming excitement, she gripped him. Declan gasped, his eyes narrowing even farther. "Feels good," he muttered. "Your hand is almost scalding."

Cole let out a ragged breath. "Just watching is overwhelming." Although, he wasn't just watching. His fingers were stroking her hips. Their movements had lifted the hem of her shirt and the tips were gliding over her flesh beneath. Wherever his hands touched, little sparks seemed to jump, making her nerves scream. The position of his fingers, toying with the band of her jeans, was suggestive.

Then, almost as if he was reading her mind, Cole pushed his hand underneath her jeans.

Zoe gave a raw gasp, her hips jerking forward in reaction. Her hand moved, sliding up Declan's shaft, coming up against the head and he made a strangled sound in his throat.

"Undo her jeans," he whispered.

Cole's spare hand snagged the button and flicked it undone. Because of the pressure of his hand beneath the zipper, he only had to lift the tab up and the zipper opened almost by itself.

He spread his fingers over her lower belly, the ends resting over her panties.

"I might come just from watching you do that," Declan said roughly. His hands were at his sides, the knuckles white, the tendons in his wrists straining.

"This?" Cole pushed his fingers under her panties and curved them around to cup her *mons*. The middle finger slipped between her lips, up against her soaked and slippery clit.

Just that light touch was enough to send a shudder of pleasure through her. She was starting to shake with it. She had to concentrate to slide her own hand the length of Declan's cock, teasing the head with her fingers. Her heart gave an extra squeeze as he moaned and his pelvis thrust.

Cole gripped the hem of her shirt with his other hand and pulled it up, until her bare breasts were revealed, the shirt rucked up over the top of the slope. She had small breasts, yet once Cole had found out how sensitive the nipples were, he rarely left them alone.

Her nipples crinkled and tightened at the touch of the air and she let her head roll back against his shoulder as Cole caught a nipple between his fingers and teased. There seemed to be a single line of nerves between her breasts and her clit, a direct connection that made any touch of her nipples extraordinarily arousing. She could feel the slickness of her pussy, the throb of her clit and the growing need to be fucked as hard as possible.

Cole lifted her off her feet, his hands around her waist. "Take her jeans," he said, his voice low.

Declan tugged on the hems and her jeans slithered off. Her socks were removed and then her panties.

"Soaked," Declan said, letting them sit on his fingers, then dropping them to the floor.

Cole's hands were pulling at the hem of her shirt again. This time, he drew it all the way off, while Declan watched, his dark eyes hot and brooding.

Cole picked her up again, this time lifting her up in his arms. He carried her over to the bed and laid her on the cover. He slithered onto the bed beside her and rested his hand on her belly.

"Declan, get your ass over here," he said, his green eyes holding Zoe's gaze.

She shivered.

Declan climbed onto the bed, on the other side from Cole. His cock jutted up from his thighs and Zoe couldn't tear her gaze away.

"Break the ice," Cole said softly.

"Finally," Declan added. He moved between her thighs and Zoe's heart tried to climb out of her chest when he picked up her knee and lifted her thigh, separating her legs.

Then he leaned over her, resting on one arm so that barely any of his weight was on her. She felt his cock against the entrance to her pussy, which pulsed in response.

"Look at me," Declan said. His voice was strained.

She met his gaze and that was when he pushed inside her. There was no resistance. She was so moist he slid all the way in and his pelvis kissed hers.

Zoe tried to breathe. Her breath shook.

Declan paused, studying her. "Wow...." He said it softly.

"Now I think I'm the one who will come just from watching," Cole murmured softly.

Zoe glanced at him. He had pushed his pajama pants down his hips, exposing his rigid cock. He was stroking it and the sight of his shaft in his own big hand made her gasp again.

"He always was a voyeur at heart," Declan said. He pulled out of her, almost the full length of his cock, then speared her again, driving himself with a power that made him groan.

Zoe tried to keep her eyes open. She wanted to watch all

of it. She wanted to watch Cole and what he was doing to himself. She wanted to watch Declan's body flexing over hers, the strain in his tendons as he fought to stave off his growing climax.

The pleasure was too intense. She thought she might fall apart with the intensity of it. It was spiraling up…and up….

She came with cry that tore at the back of her throat and for a heartbeat or two her hearing and sight faded under the power of the orgasm.

Almost before she could catch her breath, Declan rolled onto his back, bringing her with him. It drove his stiff cock deeper inside her and she gasped again.

Declan brushed the longer locks of her hair out of her eyes. "That's better," he said. He was breathing hard.

"You didn't come," she whispered.

"Not part of the agenda right now," he said. "Hold still." His hands settled on her hips.

Cole's bigger, warmer hands cupped her ass and she sucked in yet another breath of surprise.

"I do love your ass," Cole murmured.

"You said you loved mine," Declan pointed out. He didn't sound upset.

"Zoe's is better."

"Rounder, mmm…."

She looked over her shoulder. Cole had stripped off his pajamas and finally was fully naked. He was looking down at her rear, sitting between Declan's legs and hers.

As she looked around, he ran his fingers through her cleft and pressed one up against her ass.

Zoe moaned. Cole had taught her to love anal sex. She couldn't imagine how it would feel with Declan in her at the same time. She couldn't wait to find out. "Hurry," she breathed.

Cole had in his hand one of the tubes of lubricant they kept in the nightstand. "Kiss Declan," he told her. "His tongue always made me relax. See if he can do the same for you."

She looked back down at Declan, who was smiling. "He's exaggerating. He's the one who was always up for it."

"Still is," she breathed and kissed him, anyway. She moaned into his mouth as Cole's fingers spread the gel over her and into her. He pushed inside, easing the muscle and coaxing it open and her whole body responded to his touch, tightening up in anticipation. She clenched around Declan's cock and he groaned softly, his lips tearing away from hers.

Cole's fingers were replaced by his cock. The size of him was familiar to her and Zoe could almost relax, because he had taken her this way so often before. Only, Declan was beneath her this time and that made it far, far different.

Cole stroked her ass. "Let me in," he coaxed.

She deliberately drew in a deep breath and let it out and Cole pushed inside.

Zoe knew immediately that this was the perfect arrangement—the two of them inside her at once. Even before Cole eased completely into her, she could feel how wonderful it was.

She stared down at Declan, shaking with the overwhelming *rightness* of it.

"Is there anything better than this?" Declan whispered.

Zoe shook her head.

Then they both began to thrust and she knew that there was something better, after all.

She didn't get a chance to control her climax, or stretch out her pleasure. It leapt, clawing like a beast for the peak, tearing through her body as if it was a mere conduit. It blasted through her, stealing her breath and her strength.

This time, she didn't just cry out, she screamed, the guttural sound pulling from deep inside her.

Even as she shook and trembled, the climax beating at her in successive waves, she felt Cole's pace quicken and his hips to twitch as they did when he came.

Declan was straining beneath her, the tendons in his thick neck working hard. He climaxed with a groan that sounded as deep and gut wrenching as her own.

Cole rolled back onto the bed beside Declan, bringing her with him. He tucked her into the space between them, almost as if the space had been made for her.

When Zoe could breathe properly once more, she put

her hand on Declan's shoulder and looked over her own at Cole. "Why didn't we do this a long time ago?"

Chapter Eight

Alex had always had trouble looking away from Mia, even though when he had first met her, looking at her too closely was a dangerous thing. Even now, when he could look freely, he still found it hard to drag his attention away from her curves and would follow her around the room with his gaze, watching her body bend and flex, the natural grace of her movements and the overwhelmingly feminine shape of her.

He had seen hundreds of pregnant women in his time and they had never provoked any response in him except for polite acknowledgement. Now, however, he understood everything the poets and the baby-mad had been blathering about. For the first time, the baby was starting to show. It was barely even a bump, yet it was undeniably there.

His child.

Their child, for Wyatt was as fiercely happy about the baby as he was…and where was he, anyway?

Alex stirred and forced himself to look away from Mia as she moved around the kitchen area, pouring hot water, bending and stretching as she went about making herbal tea for herself. "Where is Wyatt?" he asked her. "He should have been home two hours ago."

Mia shook her head. "Beth sent a call out for any help. A vampeen breakout in Illinois. Her new trinity."

Alex got to his feet. "You let him go? He was out until three last night."

Mia halted, her lips pursed, thinning out the natural fullness. Her eyes were troubled. "I'm not the one to talk to him about it."

"Why not?"

"I'm the one who is pregnant," she said softly.

Dismay touched him. Of course, *of course*, why hadn't he realized that for himself? He had been busy—they all were these days, so that was no excuse.

The sound of a key pushing into the lock alerted them both. Mia picked up the tea cup. "I'm going to drink this in the bedroom," she said and gave him a small smile. "Be gentle."

Alex nodded.

Wyatt shut the door and bolted it, shifting the heavy duffle back over to his other hand. There was snow in his dark hair and over the shoulders of his heavy winter coat. He had been walking.

Alex waited until Wyatt turned around and saw him.

Wyatt's appearance was almost a shock. There were dark marks under his eyes and his eyes were bloodshot. Even his face had grown thinner later. Why hadn't Alex noticed before now?

Wyatt smiled at him. "You're home. Good."

"We should talk," Alex said stiffly. The shock was making it hard to speak naturally.

Wyatt's smile faded. He put the bag down and tossed his keys into the bowl on the table next to the front door. "About?"

"You."

Wyatt looked around the room. "Where's Mia?"

"Sleeping," Alex lied. "Besides, you won't hear this if she says it."

Wyatt came up to him, tilted his head and studied him. "You're doing that clipped speech thing again, Alex. What's wrong?"

"You're working too hard."

Wyatt blinked. "Isn't everyone? There are incursions all over North America these days…it's hard to keep up."

"Everyone else manages to have a life. Sort of a life," Alex amended, because none of them were really doing that. "You're pushing it to extremes, though. How much sleep are you getting these days?"

"You should know. You're next to me when I sleep." He was annoyed, now.

"I do know," Alex agreed. "I don't think I consciously noticed because I never get tired, so it didn't occur to me you weren't getting enough. Maybe four hours a night and that's on a good night. You go haring off after Grimoré and vampeen every single time anyone sends out a distress call."

"Isn't that what we're supposed to be doing?" Wyatt asked. His shoulders and face were stiff with anger.

Alex shook his head. "Not at the cost of your health."

"Why not? That's what soldiers do." This time, his temper was obvious. Wyatt crossed his arms, his feet spread. His entire well-muscled body was tight with fury. "You could be out there, too. You don't need sleep."

"Mia and you *do* and it's my job to watch over you while you sleep," Alex said, as patiently as he could. Wyatt never could process anything while his temper was roused in this way. Alex had to reach past it and there was only one way to do that. Alex braced himself. "You could kill a thousand vampeen, Wyatt. A million of them. It still won't guarantee that Mia will be safe."

Wyatt hit out, just as Alex had expected him to. Alex got his hand up and Wyatt's fist smacked into his palm. He closed his fingers around his fist and held on.

Wyatt struggled to free his arm, his face working. "What would you know about it?" he ground out.

Alex caught Wyatt's jaw in his hand, using just enough strength to make him grow still and actually look at him. "Mia isn't Julie, Wyatt. I'm here, you're here and I promise you, no one will get *near* Mia while I am standing."

Wyatt stopped struggling suddenly, all the violence and anger draining from him. His eyes glittered. "I know that," he said, his voice hoarse. "Only, these fuckers are ten times worse than the thing that killed Julie…." A single tear escaped and rolled down his cheek.

Alex drew Wyatt to him and held him. "This time you're not alone," he said quietly.

Wyatt shuddered against him. "God, Alex, I get so afraid sometimes!" His voice was muffled against Alex's shoulder. "There's more and more of them and nothing holds them back."

"We'll work it out," Alex assured him. "All of us. We'll figure it out and Mia will be safe."

It seemed to be the most natural thing in the world to lie on her side, her back against Cole's chest and listen to Declan talk. The three of them had sat up into the small hours of the night, talking just this way, many times in the past. Only, they had never been naked and never had Cole held her this way while Declan spun his tales.

Declan laid on his back and sometimes rolled onto his side to look at them. He had always been the one to tell the stories and until now, Zoe hadn't realized how much she had missed the stories and his voice falling softly. Sometimes she thought she could catch a glimpse of Irish brogue, even though Declan's family had been in Canada for generations. She had decided it was the cadences of a practiced story-teller emerging.

"Did Cole never tell you the story of how we really got together, then?" Declan asked.

She shook her head. "You told me. About the joke Valentines and how it got you both thinking."

Declan rolled into his side and raised his brow. "Then you've only heard the public version."

"That's not the way it happened?" She looked at Cole over her shoulder. "You never said anything."

Cole's jaw worked. "It's not exactly romantic," he said.

"Hell, no," Declan said. He touched the end of her nose. "You wanted to know why we never did this before now," and he waved to encompass the bed. "The whole unvarnished truth might explain it for you."

"You met in college, yes?"

Declan sighed and rolled onto his back. "We shared a house together, along with three other students. Split five ways, the rent was still crippling yet we could get by. Just. I was first year pre-med and Cole was studying computer science on his military scholarship."

"That much I know," Zoe said.

Declan rolled his head to smile at them both. "Ah, but what you don't know is that whenever we weren't studying and sometimes when we should have been, there were women."

Cole laughed. "Mild understatement."

Zoe shrugged. "I figured this out, too. You both give off those signals that make every head in the room turn when you walk in. Both male and female."

Declan propped his head on his hand. "Cole's a big, muscle-bound jock and he never failed to get laid. I didn't have much trouble, either." He grinned. "It wasn't until we both ended up in bed with the same woman that the train really got rolling."

"Oh…" Zoe breathed. "So you worked together to get women?"

Declan's smile became a mild grimace. "We didn't have to work at all. I sometimes think women have a secret telepathy and can pass on word about men. 'Avoid this jerk. That one is a prick. This guy is hung like a horse. And those two in the science division will blow your brains out if you let them.'."

Zoe laughed. "Women do talk," she admitted.

Cole sighed. "It worked, whatever it was." His fingers were trailing in lazy circles over her shoulder, dipping down toward her breast, making her replete nerves twitch and fizz.

"We fucked women like crazy," Declan said, with an utterly candid tone. "Sometimes two or three in a day. While everyone we knew was bullshitting about how much sex they were getting, Cole and I had to figure out instead how to keep up our energy to cope with it all. Good thing I was in pre-med."

Zoe's laughter was subterranean, making her shoulders shake. "What happened?"

"One of the more adventurous women said she would find it even more arousing if Cole and I kissed in front of her." Declan rested on his back, smiling with a faraway expression in his eyes. "As our motto back then was 'whatever melts her into a puddle goes,' we manned up and kissed."

He fell silent.

"You liked it," Zoe said.

"So did I," Cole said. "It was a watershed moment."

"Ay, I could see it in his eyes," Declan said and sighed. He propped himself on his elbow once more. "So we did the lady justice and sent her on her way…and that left us the rest of the night to figure out what the fuck had just happened."

"So you stopped screwing women and got together after that?" Zoe guessed.

"You're rushing the story. Hush," Declan told her. "And no, we didn't exactly stop screwing women. It was too much fun."

"Except it wasn't the same, after that," Cole added.

Declan nodded. "We both liked it well enough, except I already knew, a month after we first kissed, that Cole was the real thing for me. So having Cole in bed with me and a lady who I didn't know that well, who was just there for the fun…well, it just didn't feel right."

"That's why neither of you would make a move on me?" she asked. "Because you thought it wouldn't feel right?"

Declan looked surprised. "Are you daft?" he said hotly.

Cole tugged on her shoulder, making her roll back so she could see him properly. "It's because we knew it *would* feel right, with you of all people."

"And that would change things, all over again." Declan sighed. "Years wasted because we were too fucking scared to risk what we already had."

Zoe touched his shoulder. "It is what it is, remember?"

Declan picked up her hand and kissed the back of it. "I remember." His voice was rough.

Cole was stroking her again and she drew in a trembling breath as nerves fired and excitement flared, deep in her belly.

Declan turned his head to watch as Cole ran his hand over her, from knee to shoulder, teasing and arousing. After a while, as Zoe twitched and gasped, squirming under his hand, Declan turned on his side to watch.

"You take her," Cole said, his voice low. He flipped Zoe over and pushed her up against Declan, so that her ass was pressed against his hips. Declan steadied her hip, then teased her himself.

"Torture," she breathed, wriggling.

"Not yet," Declan told her. He pushed her top knee forward and ran his fingertips along the back of her leg.

She arched and moaned as his cock pressed up against her from behind. It was hard and insistent. He pushed into her rear entrance in slow degrees.

Cole stared into her eyes the whole time, his own filled with raw, heated lust. As Declan settled behind her, fully inside her, Cole picked up her bent knee and slid his hips beneath it.

His cock eased into her pussy and Zoe sighed at the incredible sensation it gave her to have both of them in her in this way. "And how…" she said, pausing to sip a fast breath, "are you both going to move with your hips anchored like that?"

"We don't have to," Declan said, his hand settling on her hip once more. "You're going to do all the work."

"How—oh!" She pulled in another gasp as Declan slid his hand between her body and Cole's. His fingers pushed up against her clit.

He began to stroke in firm, short touches that stole her senses and zoomed her concentration down to the pleasure building inside.

"You'll come so hard, you'll make us come, too," Declan whispered in her ear.

She didn't have the breath to spare to respond. She was almost panting and she couldn't keep still. Every muscle in her body was squeezing and her nerves screaming. As her climax built toward the peak, she saw that Cole was watching her, his face taut as the pleasure took him, too.

That made it even better.

She soared into her climax, her throat straining as she screamed silently in pleasure.

Declan's arm felt heavy over her waist, which pointed more surely toward his non-ghost status and the power of the trinity than anything else she had seen this long and strange day.

Cole's arm was laying over both her and Declan, also a deadweight.

Zoe realized she had drifted. Perhaps she had even slept for a moment. Cole's eyes were closed and she didn't want to move to check on Declan, because they were both still inside her and it was too good a sensation to disturb them and lose it.

A tiny face was peering at her from over Cole's big shoulder.

Zoe parted her lips and very nearly spoke. Then she remembered something that Diego had said about Lindal, the elvish prince in the first trinity.

She closed her mouth again and spoke in her mind in firm, loud words. *Are you looking for protection?*

That had been the primary concern of the little pixie who had attached herself to Lindal.

As soon as she "spoke", the little thing flickered over Cole's shoulder, her wings fluttering. She hung in midair between Cole and Zoe, just above Zoe's face. Images and feelings came at Zoe, appearing in her mind is if they were her own thoughts. Yet they were alien and carried information she had not known until now.

"Someone is coming," she said, struggling to sit up.

The pixie, a tiny woman in a silvery dress, was flitting around now. Excitement and agreement came from her, mixed up with a fear that was directed beyond the house.

Cole stirred.

"Blessed Mary Mother," Declan said. "Pixies. So they really do exist."

"Hey!" Cole said. There was a second pixie tugging on his hair, trying to get him to sit up. "I'm coming, I'm coming," he muttered.

Suddenly, the air over the bed was filled with little creatures fluttering and hovering anxiously.

Zoe waved at them, trying to move them out of the way. Their combined distress and anxiousness that the big people rise to meet the threat coming their way forced her off the bed, to scramble for her jeans and shirt. Cole strode over to the closet and pulled out a pair of work jeans.

Declan looked around the floor. "Hell. What do I do

now?" he asked. His clothes had disappeared when he had dropped them.

One of the pixies hovered in front of him.

"What?" he said. Then his brow lifted. "I see." He stood still, looking into middle distance and suddenly, he was dressed again. This time, in a shirt and jeans that Zoe also remembered from before. He tugged at the waistband of the jeans. "That's a time-saver," he said. "Especially if it works in the opposite direction." And he looked at her and winked.

Zoe grinned. "I don't know which of you two is the worst."

"Declan is!" Cole called back over his shoulder as he opened the bedroom door, already striding to meet whatever the threat was.

"Definitely Cole," Declan added.

Chapter Nine

They hurried down the front stairs, accompanied by the fluttering pixies. Diego was standing at the front door with a gun in his hand, looking up at them as they descended. "There's someone coming," he said. "Big, black truck with lights on the cab."

Cole glanced through the pane and sighed. "It's Brady."

Zoe bit her lip.

"My brother? *That* Brady?" Declan asked.

"How many Bradys do you know?" Cole asked.

"He's changed, since you died," Zoe added.

Declan frowned. "The house, right? I gave it to Cole and he thinks it belongs to the family, even though I built the damn thing."

"That's about the size of it," Cole said heavily. He looked at Diego's gun. "You won't need that. He's a reasonable man. Mostly."

"Generally, he might be. Only, I want to know how he got through the blockade," Diego replied. "There isn't a scratch or dent on the truck that I can see and I can see a long way."

"They let him through?" Zoe said. "Why would they do that?"

"We're about to find out," Diego said. "Declan, you should leave." From the outside came the sound of sharply applied brakes, the tires skidding in the gravel. The rumbling engine turned off.

"I want to see him!" Declan said.

Boots crunched on the gravel and climbed up the stairs.

"You can't. We don't reveal ourselves to the normal world," Zoe said, speaking quietly, for they were all gathered close by the front door. As she spoke, Brady's figure crossed the space visible through the pane on the left side of the door and she drew back, startled.

"He's my brother," Declan said hotly. He spoke in a harsh whisper.

"Right now, he might not be," Diego said. His voice was normal and touched with impatience. "Be a good boy and fuck off for a few minutes until we figure out why he's here and how he got through."

Declan's lips parted in surprise.

The front door was shoved open. Brady didn't knock, or ring the bell. He just turned the handle and pushed.

Everyone jumped backward, shocked.

Brady strode through the opening and came to a halt just beyond the door, looking as startled as they were.

Zoe glanced at Declan. He had disappeared. He wasn't

in the hallway and he hadn't had time to move into one of the other rooms, not even if he had sprinted and they would have surely heard that.

Where was he?

Something squeezed her hand and Zoe sucked in a breath.

Declan. He actually *had* disappeared.

No one noticed Zoe's surprise. They were all focused upon Brady.

As Declan did, Brady had Black Irish features and a temper to go with it. He was a physical man, with a slightly bigger build than Declan. However, he also liked to drink and his belly and extra fat made him slow on his feet.

Yet all the Stewart family was intellectually brilliant. They had produced generations of doctors and lawyers, scientists and thinkers, plus the odd politician or two. All of them had added to the family's wealth and power. Brady ran his own construction company and after the death of Declan's father only a year before Declan's, Brady had nominated himself the head of the family. He wanted to preserve the family legacy and that included the big house that Declan had built.

Cole had been in an endless legal battle with Brady since Declan had died and the few times they had met face to face had been tense and unpleasant. Cole wasn't about to give up the home where he and Declan had lived so happily just because Brady had an overblown sense of family and a distaste for the gender of Declan's spouse.

Brady didn't look irritated now. He looked mad and not just angry-mad. He had been drinking. Zoe could smell the booze from where she stood by the bottom of the stairs. His eyes were bloodshot and his face was working with fury.

He looked around at the three of them in the hall that he could see. "I'd have words with you, Pasternak."

"Did you see anything among the trees when you drove through them?" Cole asked.

Brady blinked. He shifted on his feet, swaying a little. "I've come to take the house back." He spoke as if he was reciting words that he had rehearsed. "It rightfully belongs to the Stewarts, not a man like you."

"Except Declan didn't leave the house to the family," Cole said. "Brady, this is such an old argument. When are you going to give up on it? The law is on my side. No judge will ever break the will."

"Silence," Diego said. He stood with his head down and turned, his eyes narrowed. He was listening to something no one else could hear.

Except Zoe could hear it. Snuffles and growls and other... "Voices," she said. "I can hear voices out there."

Diego drew his other gun. "Vampeen," he said. "They're building up. Preparing."

"Is that guns?" Brady said. He turned to look at Diego

fully. "I don't know you."

Diego gave him a hard smile. "Who did you talk to out there? Who said it would be a good idea for you to come and argue with your brother's husband?"

Brady frowned. "How did you know…" Then his frown cleared. "Oh, right," he muttered and reached inside his open coat. He moved fast, even as drunk as he was. Zoe had seen Declan in the same state more than once in the past and both brothers seemed to have an infinite capacity for alcohol. It had never slowed Declan down too much, either.

"Gun!" Cole cried. His hand slammed into Zoe's shoulder and she staggered away from him, pin wheeled her arms as her balance tottered. She pressed a hand into the floor to regain her balance and push herself back upright.

The sound of a gun firing in the foyer was incredibly loud.

Zoe screamed and crouched down, flinching.

"Where did he go?" Brady demanded.

The acrid smell of smoke and cordite made Zoe's throat close up and her eyes to sting. She turned to look.

Cole was not where he had been standing, which was where Brady was aiming the pistol.

Diego snatched the gun out of his hand and pushed him backward, toward the corner of the hall. "*Who did you talk to?*"

"Cole!" Zoe cried.

"Here. I'm here," Cole said.

She looked up at the top of the stairs. Cole was climbing down them and she threw herself forward to meet him. "God, I thought he'd shot you!"

Cole held her. He was shaking, too. "I'm not sure what happened. I saw the muzzle then suddenly, I was back in the bedroom."

Diego had his hand around Brady's throat. He jerked his chin around to look at Cole. "You teleported? *You?* It's supposed to…" Then he sighed. "It's generally the woman or one of the women of the trinity who can jump. You're the first man, apart from the elf, and he could always do that."

Zoe frowned. "Then what am I supposed to be?" she asked.

Diego looked at her sharply. "You heard the vampeen."

Brady was watching them with his red eyes, a faintly puzzled air about him. "What's a trinity?" he asked.

Diego gave him a little shake. "Tell me who you spoke to."

Brady blinked slowly again. "Spoke?"

"Who told you to come here?"

"I…just wanted to," Brady said. "I'm allowed."

"Who did you speak to on the way here?" Diego demanded.

"Maybe he really did come here on his own volition," Cole said. "He's done it before."

"Not through that pack of things out there," Diego said with flat certainty. "He was wound up by someone and aimed at you. I told you they would try to break up the trinity before the bond was sealed. They figured out your brother is someone you would open the door to."

Zoe's throat seemed to tighten once more. "You mean...they've been *studying* us?"

"Military intelligence. I would have done my research if I had been them, too," Cole said quietly.

"The white-faced dude," Brady said suddenly.

They looked at him. "What about him?" Diego said and gave him another little shake. Even though Brady was taller than Diego, it still looked like a dog dealing with a caught rabbit.

"He kept whispering and whispering. Lips never bloody moved. Only I couldn't get the words out of my head...." Brady wiped the back of his hand over his mouth. "Even shooting him didn't stop it."

"*You shot it?*" Cole said.

Diego hauled Brady out of the corner and pushed him toward Cole. "Is there a bedroom you can lock him in, where he can sleep it off? We're not going to get anything coherent out of him and we don't have time, anyway."

Cole gripped Brady's arm.

"Try jumping there with him," Diego said shortly, pulling out his phone. "If you're the jumper, then it's your job to take passengers."

Cole raised a brow. Then he looked at Brady. "Here goes…" he said.

Abruptly, neither of them were there.

From upstairs came a sound that Zoe had heard more than once as a medical assistant. Someone was vomiting.

"Oh, for the love of Pete!" Cole bellowed, from the same direction.

Diego laughed. "Wish I'd seen that," he murmured and dialed. "Yeah…Beth. We've got a development. You'd better come."

Zoe could hear the woman's voice on the other end of the phone, even though she was standing by the bottom of the stairs still.

"Who?" Beth asked.

"Everyone," Diego said simply. He looked at the air next to Zoe. "You, too, Declan."

Declan appeared, standing next to her. "How did you know I was here?"

"You're covered in pixie dust. I can smell it," Diego said shortly. He spoke into the phone. "Sooner the better, Seaveth."

* * * * *

The room was full of people Zoe didn't know, which generally made her uneasy until she had mentally catalogued them, figured out names and the degree of danger they might represent. The old mental habits of hunting were coming back in a rush. Despite her caution among a group of strangers, Zoe found she was looking back at the mantelshelf over the fireplace, her gaze pulled there by fascination.

Among the photos and knickknacks were at least eight pixies that she could see. They were tiny people, both male and female, although even the males seemed delicate, with their gossamer wings and ageless faces.

They were sitting, standing, leaning and hovering among the photos, listening to the big people and talking among themselves. Their talking was almost silent, highlighted by the high-pitched trilling they made.

One of them had arrived with the man—the elf—called Lindal. He was astonishingly tall, with limpid blue eyes that reminded Zoe of the woman who had brought Diego his guns. There was a relationship there, she suspected.

The woman was here, too, sitting next to Diego, her hand in his. Sera. Another elf.

The other woman in the room was Seaveth. She was statuesque, with masses of red curls that tumbled down her back to brush her ass as she moved. There was absolutely no doubt that she was the leader in the room. Everyone was looking at her or deferred to her. Everyone listened carefully when she spoke, as she was doing now.

"If they influenced Declan's brother, it must have been some sort of mental domination," Seaveth said, "as you say he wasn't under physical stress, if you discount the effects of the liquor."

"That's a new trick," said the man standing behind Diego and Sera. He had dirty blonde hair and stood with his arms crossed. Zoe pegged him as some sort of law enforcement, based on the stance alone. "I wonder from how far away they can exert the influence? We've never really gotten close to one of them before."

"Blake's right." The dark-haired man sitting next to Lindal said. "They use the vampeen as a barricade. If there is a wounded one out there, we should go find it."

"Just getting close would give us a lot of information about them," Seaveth said in agreement.

"If it is wounded, it will need help," Declan said. He didn't speak particularly loudly, yet everyone turned to look at him. He was wearing the jeans and tee shirt Zoe had first seen him in. They were what he had reappeared in and she wondered if that was his default clothing. Would he always be wearing them, if he didn't consciously choose to appear in something else?

"Medical help," Declan said, clarifying himself.

Diego shook his head. "Let the fucker die," he said harshly. "You don't know what these things have done. What they're capable of doing." He glanced at Blake.

Blake's jaw rippled. "They're heartless," he said, his voice low. "They've already used your brother against you and Cole, and that's mild."

Zoe wondered who it was they had used against him.

"So we should be heartless just because they are?" Declan asked, heat in his voice.

Seaveth held up her hand. "First things first. Let's see if there is a wounded Grimoré out there. It's possible his colleagues have already dealt with him in whatever manner they use for their wounded." She looked at Diego. "I would ask Blake to hunt, except that in this case, I think he should remain here with Cole, Zoe and Declan. Zack can hunt with you, if you are in agreement."

Diego shrugged. "I was a hunter a long time before Blake was dubbed."

"Which is why I'm asking. Thank you."

Zoe got to her feet. "Wait, why can't we come?"

Seaveth shook her head. "Your trinity has not been sealed yet. You're incredibly vulnerable right now. If something happened to one of you before the seal was made, I don't know what that would do to weaken our ranks. Each trinity is critical, each is precious to us. You must remain behind and complete the bonding."

"Fine by me," Declan said heavily.

Cole shook his head. "I know the woods out there. So does Zoe. So does Declan, better than me. We should come with you. There are more than enough of us, even against these hounds and things."

"Vampeen," Diego said. "Don't discount them. You've yet to meet one."

"They're human, you said," Cole shot back.

"They were human, once," Sera said quietly. "They are no longer human. The conversion process destroys nearly everything they once were." She reached up and took Blake's hand.

"If they were once human, they have human limitations in strength and speed," Cole said. "That makes them predictable."

Diego's smile was wise. "Okaaaay," he said and looked at Seaveth. "If you let him go, I want to be next to him when he meets his first vampeen. With a camera, too."

"I'm not letting him go," Seaveth said firmly. "I'm sorry, Cole. Zoe. We simply cannot risk you at this time. We have three hunters and we're all used to combing among trees for them. We'll manage."

Zoe sat back down again. There was ruthless sense in what she was saying.

Cole shook his head. He stayed silent. He wasn't going to argue anymore, either.

"That just leaves finding the sucker," Diego said. "I've never smelled them before. Vampeen, yes. I've never been close enough to learn a Grimoré's scent. Zack?"'

Zack shook his head.

Seaveth smiled. "Yesterday, I couldn't find my keys. I mean, it wasn't simply that I'd left them somewhere other than the pot by the door and I just had to look around quickly to find them again. They'd fallen down behind the bed and were on the floor beneath it. I wouldn't have thought to look there in a million years. After I had spent a couple of minutes of looking in all the usual places, Ferr came to me and led me right to them."

"You asked her?" Lindal said, his tone curious.

"She just seemed to know." Seaveth's gaze swiveled toward the mantelshelf.

"Be careful how you ask," Lindal said quietly. "Remember how Ferr reacts to anything she doesn't like."

"They disappear?" Zoe guessed, looking at the pixies moving around on the shelf.

"They jump away," Lindal confirmed.

"Emphasize the wounded quality. The helplessness of the Grimoré," Seaveth said.

Lindal moved closer to the shelf and looked down at the little creatures. He didn't speak, yet all of them looked up at him, startled, as if he had shouted.

Some of them cowered next to their friends, holding each other. Yet, none of them vanished.

Sera got to her feet and came and stood with Lindal and now Zoe could see without question the family resemblance.

They were most likely brother and sister.

Both of them stood and "spoke".

The trilling and cooing among the pixies leapt in volume. They all flew into the air, circling around Lindal and Sera.

"I think that's a yes," Lindal said.

Three of the pixies headed toward the living room doorway out into the front hall and as they flew, golden sparkles floated out behind them.

"Trails," Cole said. "They're laying down breadcrumbs for us to follow."

Zoe watched the slowly sinking trail of dust, a strong sense of familiarity gripping her. "I wonder if Walt Disney was a part of the supernatural world," she said. "That would explain a lot."

Seaveth looked at her, startled. "Oh, that would just ruin my childhood memories!"

"So they can make up stories about vampires all day long, they just aren't allowed to destroy your illusions about fairies?" Zack asked. He rolled his eyes. "Come on, let's get this done." He started to follow the pixies and Diego, Seaveth and Lindal moved with him. Even Sera was zipping up the heavy coat she wore.

Blake dropped onto the sofa where Diego had been sitting with a heavy sigh.

Everyone who was going on the hunt moved out into

the hallway after the pixies in the lead, while the rest of the pixies followed. That left Cole and Declan standing by Zoe, with Blake on the sofa. Zoe heard the front door open.

"Why have they stopped?" Zack said.

"Hey! Don't go!" Diego said.

Suddenly, the air in front of Cole and Zoe and Declan was full of pixies, hovering and flitting around their heads. Zoe ducked as one almost flew into her face.

Even Blake was batting at them.

Seaveth walked back into the room and watched.

Zoe stared at the little one hovering in front of her nose. The lady was anxious and.... "Stubborn," Zoe breathed. She focused on Seaveth, by the door. "They won't go unless we do."

"Lindal? Sera?" Seaveth called over her shoulder without moving.

"That's what we're understanding, too," Sera called back.

Seaveth sighed. "Then you'd better come, too," she told Zoe. "Bring every weapon you've got and if you happen to have full body armor, I'd prefer you wear that, too."

Chapter Ten

Declan "changed" his clothes by thinking it through, although Zoe suspected he would be impervious to the cold... if he could even move far beyond the house. "You have to be ready to be jerked back to the house, if you get too far beyond it," she told him.

"Anchored by my remains?" he asked.

"Your ashes are here?" she asked, startled. Cole had wanted to take care of the spreading of Declan's ashes and had got his way over the protests of the family. Zoe had let him take care of them by himself, his last private moment with Declan. He had never told her where he had put them.

"Out in the back garden," Cole said shortly. He was concentrating on checking the loading of a pistol that Blake had handed him.

Declan had refused any weapons offered to him. Diego had pushed one of his pistols into Zoe's hand. "You're the hunter, I suspect. You'd be better with a knife. We all are. There's just none to spare right now."

"A pistol is fine," she said and snapped out the clip and checked it, then pushed it back.

Cole stared at her. So did Declan.

"What?" she demanded.

"Nothing," Cole said. "I just…." He shrugged.

"We're both used to seeing you in scrubs, with nothing more lethal than a scalpel," Declan added.

"They're getting impatient!" Diego called from the front door.

Zoe went through to the crowded hallway to get her coat and boots. There were even more people there now, including a tall red-headed man and another with heavy muscles. And one with grey in his hair, a gold badge on his belt and trousers with stripes down the legs, although his coat was civilian normal.

There was yet another woman with them. Blonde, with brown eyes.

All the newcomers were staring at Declan with intense curiosity in their faces.

"Introductions later," Diego said shortly. He opened the door and the pixies zipped through it in a quick stream and were gone.

The trail the pixies left behind them was unmistakable, so even though they had moved far ahead of them, no one was worried about missing the direction. They moved in a pack, with Zoe, Cole and Declan in the middle, per Seaveth's orders. They went on foot, pushing through the knee-high, powdering snow across the two acres of cleared land in front of the house.

Zoe kept glancing at Declan to assure herself he was still here. He gave her a stiff smile. "I would rather jump back to the house," he said softly, "and sit this out. I just don't think the little ones will let me."

One of the pixies appeared in front of him, chittering. The chiding tone was unmistakable.

"I guess not," Cole said, sounding amused.

"I think they know more about the limits of my presence here than I do, so far," Declan added.

"It can be like that in the underworld," Zoe said. "We all know of each other. We know our strengths and weaknesses. It makes us better hunters."

Declan looked unhappy. "I suppose."

"Although, so far, you're defying everything I know about spirits," Zoe added.

He didn't speak again.

The direction the pixies were taking them was to the west, into the wildness area between the mountains and the main highway that ran almost due east into Revelstoke.

"There's twenty-five hundred hectares of untouched land between the house and the secondary road that runs out to the ski hill," Cole said.

"What's that in miles?" Diego said impatiently.

"One hundred square miles, almost," the red-headed man said.

"Then I'm glad they know where they're going," Zack added, for the pixies were flying unerringly in one direction.

They moved into the trees and the light, which had already begun to fade toward sunset, dropped even farther.

Zoe blinked, looking around as they moved on. "I can see," she said.

Cole looked at her, puzzled.

Diego hopped over a branch with lithe power. "You're the hunter," he said shortly. "You can probably see as I can. Everything is very clear, in shades of gray?"

She nodded.

"Can you smell that muskiness?" he asked.

She sniffed and coughed. "Oh, ugh…"

"I can't smell anything," Cole said.

"Nor me. That's to be expected," Declan said.

"That's the scent of the vampeen," Diego said grimly. "From its strength I can tell they're less than a mile away."

Cold fingers walked up Zoe's back. She gripped the pistol, which was sitting in the band of her jeans.

"Silence," Seaveth said firmly.

They moved on.

As they progressed, Zoe got the sensation there were others on either side of them, shadowing their movements through the trees. She tried to look, only the failing daylight in here was thick with shadows and dark spots. Even with her newly improved vision, it still felt more as if she was imagining the dark shapes, than seeing them.

Diego touched her arm and jerked his chin to one side, then to the other.

Then it wasn't her imagination. She nodded at him.

The disgusting, pungent scent of the vampeen grew stronger, until Zoe found she was constantly swallowing and breathing through her mouth to lessen the impact. It was a warning scream, making her slow down and try to monitor every direction, even behind her.

While everyone in the group moved very quietly through the trees, they weren't completely silent. The untouched snow, which was much thinner in here, still crunched under their feet and the leaf litter and twigs beneath shifted, too.

Zoe could hear beyond them, into the forest itself. There was movement there. She could hear stealthy steps, the padding of feet that wore no shoes. Among them, though, were other steps. Heavier ones.

The pixies didn't hesitate. In the gloaming, their trail shone and glittered, fading slowly. They would zoom ahead, then circle back encouragingly. Their chittering and calling had ceased, but they didn't slow or change direction. They knew exactly where they were going.

Overhead, the sky Zoe could glimpse between the trees was darkening.

"God, that smell!" someone whispered.

Now the non-hunters were able to smell the vampeen, too.

"We're close," Seaveth said.

"We're not alone," Zoe warned her.

The pixies suddenly chittered in excitement, bouncing in the air to draw their attention. They were circling around a spot just ahead, on the other side of smaller bushes that were merely a darker shape in the low light.

The howl broke out, not far to their right. Everyone gave startled sounds or sucked in their breath. It might have been a dog or wolf howling, except Zoe knew no natural creature had ever made that tortured, evil sound.

More howling joined the first, then another to their left.

The hounds were all around them.

"Tighten up," Seaveth said calmly. "Stay alert. Keep moving."

"They'll rush us," Diego said grimly.

Zachary, who was at the head of the thick column of people, halted on the other side of the bushes. "Fuck me!" he said, his voice low.

Everyone pushed forward to see what he had spotted.

Zoe took her gun out. The skin on the back of her neck was prickling almost painfully and cold waves were rolling over her shoulders. Her heart was thundering.

There was something lying on the ground at Zack's feet.

The creature had pulled itself up so it was resting up against the trunk of a tree, hemmed in by the thick bushes on either side. It had found a hole to hide in and lick its wounds.

She guessed that standing on its feet, it would be over seven feet tall. Yet it was skinnier than Sera, who was the most petite person in the group besides Zoe. The only part of the creature showing above the dank garb it was wearing was its face. It was a sickly pale white color and looked damp. The elongated features had small eyes and the lids were closed. There were holes where the nose would be and a mouth that had no lips and was half the size of a human's. There were no ears that she could see. The head was long, the forehead rising up like a dome. There was no hair.

The creature was filthy, black and smelly. The aroma was like the worst of spoiled food and rotting meat together.

Zoe gasped, bending over, as illness swamped her. "That smell isn't its clothes at all," she whispered. "It's the thing itself!"

Cole patted her shoulder. "I can catch a whiff of it if I breathe hard, so I'm not."

There was a different scent underneath the rottenness. It was sharp and oily. "I think it's bleeding," she said. "I can smell it."

"That burning oil smell?" Blake said. "It's lying in it."

"Let me get at him," Declan said firmly. "Let me see."

The sound of creatures crashing through the trees at a

great pace came all around them. Zoe whirled.

"They're coming!" Diego cried and fired off his pistol. Zoe heard a heavy body land. She was already firing her own pistol, the spare clip in her left hand, ready to slap in.

There were dog-like creatures and more human types that ran on two legs. Both of them had inhuman faces. Their crooked, sharply pointed teeth were bared as they rushed them.

The others pressed in front of Zoe, shielding her.

Declan tugged on her arm. "Help me get him out from among the bushes. I have reach him."

Zoe stared at him. Even in the heat of battle, he was focused upon helping those in need.

She whirled again as someone cried out. She wasn't used to her enhanced vision and blinked to make sense of what she was seeing. Zack was on his back, his arms up and his hands around the neck of one of the hound creatures, which was snapping at his face with its vicious teeth.

As she looked, Diego squeezed, growling with the effort. The hound slumped and grew still and he tossed it away.

Shadows pushed into the space that had opened up when Diego had fallen. They raced through the weak spot. Everyone on the perimeter was fighting off more of them.

The big hounds came straight at Cole, who was nearest. They leapt up and he fired the gun into the face of the closest. It was thrown aside by the impact of the bullets.

The second landed on Cole's chest, knocking him down. More black shapes rushed toward him.

"Declan!" Zoe screamed. She shot the nearest hound, then kicked at it, trying to get the body out of her way. She had to reach Cole.

Declan spun around from the wounded Grimoré, his eyes wide.

Zoe started to kick and hit the creatures around Cole. She fired her last bullet into the nearest head, reloaded and started hauling. She forgot to guard her back. She didn't care.

There was a high whistling sound as a heavy branch from the nearest tree whipped through the air, almost as if it was sweeping a table clear. The hounds and vampeen trying to get to Cole were slapped away and sent rolling and sprawling, one of them whimpering in pain.

Zoe looked up, startled.

A slender man or woman was standing just beside the trunk of the tree. There was another on the other side of the trunk, hauling back on the limb of the tree with more strength than such a slight creature could be expected to have. They looked directly at her, then let the branch go. It whipped through the air just as the first one had. More of the vampeen were swept away.

The first lithe creature sprang over to where Cole laid and tried to haul on his shoulder. So did Zoe. She picked up his arm and dragged him to the tree the little man had been standing next to.

A vampeen leapt at her with a snarl of teeth and she dropped Cole's arm and fired calmly, dropping it to the ground.

Declan was staring at her, frozen. Then he straightened with a jerk and pointed. "Behind you!" he yelled.

Then, abruptly, he wasn't there anymore.

She heard an odd coughing sound behind her and whirled.

Declan was there and there was a vampeen at his feet. As she looked, he reached out and touched the second one on the shoulder as it leapt toward her. It dropped to the ground as though it had been clubbed and lay still.

Declan lifted his hands and looked at them. Horror formed in his face.

"Hurry! Around them!" someone shouted.

The trinities coalesced around them once more, a barrier against the vampeen.

Declan dropped to his knees next to Cole. "Let me see," he said, trying to pull Cole's hands away from his stomach.

"Why are they backing off?" Diego cried.

"They know their work is done," Declan said bitterly.

Cole was breathing in harsh little pants. As the forest grew still around them, the creatures moving back into the shadows, Cole moaned in pain.

Zoe kneeled next to him and looked at Declan. "Help him."

Declan closed his eyes. "His liver is gone," he whispered.

Zoe knew what that meant. No one could survive without a liver.

Diego crouched next to them.

So did the red-headed man. "Seal the trinity. Now, before it's too late," he said urgently. "You've joined in body already, haven't you?"

Zoe stared at him, just barely putting together his meaning.

"Yes, they have," Diego said firmly. He picked up Zoe's wrist and pulled his upper lip back. His fangs descended.

The red-head picked up Declan's. "I don't even know if this will work on you," he said to Declan.

"What are you doing…oh!" Zoe breathed as Diego bit into her wrist. She could feel him tearing the skin back. It didn't hurt because all she could feel was overwhelming lust. She wanted to fuck him…anyone…*someone*. Her body screamed for physical release.

Distantly, she felt Diego tugging on her wrist.

"Drink," he said and pressed something against her lips.

She refocused. It was Declan's wrist he was holding, while the other vampire was pushing her wrist toward Declan. She could see blood dripping from her wrist. Declan's, though, showed an open wound, with only darkness beyond.

"I don't know how this works, yet it must," Diego said. "Put your mouth on it and draw whatever you can into your mouth. Then you must swallow it."

She tried. Declan's flesh was still not-hot, not-cold. She put her lips over the small break in his skin and sucked. Her eyes widened. There was nothing in her mouth. She could feel that. Yet at the same time, there was *something* there. She swallowed, even though there was nothing to swallow. She felt it move back into her throat and pass downward.

Diego was watching her closely.

"There *was* something," she said.

"Now Cole," he said. "You'll have to guide him. He must drink from both of you, before he fades."

Her arousal was diminishing. Pain in her wrist helped her focus.

Declan was drawing her blood into his mouth.

The red-haired vampire was biting into Cole's wrist. "Sorry," he murmured to Cole. He brought the bleeding wrist up to Declan. "Cole, too," he said.

Declan nodded.

"Give your wrist to Cole," Diego told her. "Make him drink."

She dropped down lower, so that she was right next to Cole's head. His panting had dropped to shallow breaths and he was watching her with pain-filled eyes. Zoe touched his cheek, hiding her own despair. "You must drink this. Just a sip, Cole. Then we can take care of you."

He tried to speak. The only sound that emerged was a formless one of pain.

Zoe blinked back her tears furiously and pressed her wrist against his lips. "Drink," she whispered. "Two little sips and this will all be over. Even the pain."

His lips moved weakly against hers.

"I don't think he has the strength," she whispered, fear blossoming in her.

"I can fix that, temporarily. Make it fast when he rouses," the red-haired man said. He picked Cole up and tilted his head to one side, then bit down into his neck.

Cole's eyes widened and he moaned. It wasn't a sound of pain, but of a man deep in the throes of passion.

"Quickly," Diego directed her.

Startled, Zoe pressed her wrist up against Cole's mouth once more. She felt him drawing in her blood, in a deep sip. "And swallow," she reminded him.

His throat worked.

"Declan," Diego said, with a snap in his voice.

Declan put his wrist against Cole's mouth. "Drink, Cole," he breathed.

Zoe could see his throat moving as he swallowed whatever essence it was that they had drawn from Declan's spirit.

"Now you," Diego said, bringing Cole's dripping wrist

toward her. "Last one, then it's my turn."

"Your turn?"

"He's being euphemistic," the other vampire said. "Quickly. There's not much time."

The urgency in his voice was unmistakable. Zoe sucked, drawing Cole's blood. She swallowed quickly.

"It's done?" she asked. "The bond is sealed?"

Howling broke out all around them, along with more inhuman sounds. It seemed as though every dark creature among the trees gave throat to a scream of protest.

Diego grinned. "What do you think?"

"Jump! Jump!" Seaveth cried. "Before they attack again. Take as many as you can!"

"Take the body!" Declan shouted, leaping to his feet. He hurried over to the prone Grimoré and tugged on the feet. "We must take it."

Around them, the air shivered as many, many more people appeared among the trees and all around them. They wore cloaks, the hoods up. One landed almost right next to Zoe. She saw big eyes, that reminded her of Lindal and Sera.

The man put his arms around her and she felt him strain upwards. The trees and the thick night air vanished and were replaced by a large room with concrete walls and floor and nothing else in it.

There were dozens of the hooded men in the room, each with an arm around one of the people who had been in the forest with them.

Even Cole was in the arms of one of them and now, in this normal, bright light, she could see the great wound that had torn up his torso, almost all the way up to the top of his chest.

Diego grabbed the arm of the one carrying Cole. "This way. Quickly. Hurry up." He pulled the cloaked man out of the room.

The rest of the cloaked men were vanishing, jumping away again. Zoe turned to look at the one that had brought her here. He was already gone.

"That's elves for you," Seaveth said with a smile. "Silent efficiency."

"Where are they taking Cole?" Zoe demanded.

Declan appeared next to her and looked around. "Woah!" He put his hand out, as if he was trying to balance.

Seaveth looked at him curiously.

"So, there is a limitation to where I can go, after all," he told her.

"You're in New York. It's not a very tight limit," Seaveth said.

"Zoe is here. So is Cole. That's my limit," he said. "As soon as you all disappeared, I was pulled back to the house. Then I could *feel* Zoe, pulling me here...." He looked around. "Where is Cole?"

Seaveth gave them both a warm smile. "You won't be

able to see him for a while. He will be fine, though."

Zoe pressed her lips together. *My turn next*, Diego had said.

"He just won't be human any more, will he?" she said.

Seaveth's smile faded. "No. Cole's time as a human is at an end."

Declan sighed. "We saved the trinity?"

"We did," she agreed. "I don't know if this will give you any comfort at all. It seems the force that arranges the trinities, that anticipated the coming of the Grimoré, also predicted this would happen, too. There is always at least one vampire in every trinity and I thought yours was the anomaly. I didn't know how you would seal the bond...yet it seems you have ended up exactly where you should be."

She waved toward the doors at the end of the room. "Come. We have food, fresh clothing and showers. It's time to meet the other trinities."

Chapter Eleven

Zack's kiss on her cheek caught Beth mid-yawn, disrupting it completely. "Bed time, sleepyhead," he said, picking up her hand. "You've righted the world, saved the trinities and reunited the lovers. The war will still be here when you wake up tomorrow."

"There's something bothering you, isn't there?" Lindal asked. He was standing at the window, watching wet snow slide down the glass and melt.

Beth sighed. It had been a busy night. They had introduced Zoe and Declan to everyone, while Diego had whipped Cole away to an isolated place where he could ease him through the transition to vampire. Zoe had looked pale while they explained to her what they were doing, but as she had been surrounded by vampires at the time and had been in the business once herself, she didn't raise the sort of objections a human coming in cold might have done.

Declan had merely shrugged. "Cole and Zoe can handle me being what I am. I'm the last one to scream about Cole not being human anymore."

Wyatt and Alexander had pulled Beth over to a spare

table in the dining room not long after that. Wyatt had a map of North America that he spread out on the table in front of her. "I took some time off hunting the bastards and did some hard thinking instead," Wyatt said and glanced up at Alex, who smiled and rested his hand on Wyatt's shoulder.

Wyatt leaned over the map. "I talked to the shifter… Gilbert, the bear soul from the north that Diego brought in."

Beth nodded.

"He's very old. Older than he looks," Wyatt added. "He's got a lot of memories. But it's the recent stuff he recalls that was interesting." He spread his hand over the map. "I think the Grimoré are only in North America."

"That's something we've suspected for a while," Beth said. "None of the hunters in other countries have reported anything suspicious and after all these years they know what to look for." She was in endless communication with the worried groups in Europe and Asia and in the south, too.

"I think there's a reason they haven't spread too far," Wyatt said. He tapped the map again. "I talked to Sera and Lindal tonight, too. They told me some interesting things about the bridge between the elven world and ours. Did you know that if you can't teleport the way elves can do, when you come across the bridge, you land in the same place on Earth every single time?"

"Where?" Alex asked curiously.

"Southern France," Wyatt said.

"Lucky. It could have been in the middle of the Pacific," Alex murmured.

"Anyway, as everyone using *that* bridge can teleport, they can emerge from the bridge and jump to wherever they want, so it doesn't make a lick of difference to the elves."

"But the Grimoré can't teleport," Beth breathed.

Wyatt pointed to her. "Right." He tapped the map again. "I used an old hunter thing. I tracked sightings and reports, every single incident, and put them on the map." He took his hand away. "The lighter colors are older sightings. Darker are more recent. Can you see the pattern?"

Beth studied the map. She put her fingers over New York. "It started right here."

Wyatt nodded. "I think the Grimoré bridge to Earth is somewhere in New York state."

Alex blew out his breath. "Hell's bells, if we could shut down the gate…"

Beth frowned, staring down at the map. "They went north and south and west…they scattered. Look, they're everywhere."

"That was something that Gilbert pointed out to me," Wyatt said. He put both hands around the big cloud of crosses and check marks, right at the top of the map. "The sightings stop here, south of the Arctic circle. Then they

140

start moving south again. That's why Gilbert was pushing south. He was running ahead of them." Wyatt sat back. "It's October. Winter is coming in," he added.

Beth sat back, too. "They don't like the cold."

"No, they don't like it at all," Wyatt agreed, smiling. "So now we know why they've moving and where they're heading."

"South," Beth said, feeling a surge of deep satisfaction.

That had been the last big revelation in a night filled with them. Beth looked at Zack and Lindal now, feeling the edge of excitement touch her again, despite her tiredness.

"I keep thinking about how precisely this whatever-it-is seems to have anticipated everything that happens," she told them. "Gilbert's wisdom. Wyatt's map. A possible location for the bridge the Grimoré are using to get here. Cole's death. That he would be turned and would become the vampire of the trinity. That Declan would refuse to fight and we would find our doctor in him."

Lindal nodded. "Are you going to let him autopsy the Grimoré we found?"

"There's no harm that can come from it," Beth said, "and we might just learn something useful. So yes, I will, once we've all recovered and put tonight far behind us. I know no one said anything, yet Cole's death impacted every trinity. I could see it in their faces."

"I felt it, too," Zack murmured. "If we had not sealed

the trinity first, if we hadn't been able to turn him, we would have been permanently weakened. It was like having a prop pulled out from under us. We were, for a little while there, all balancing on one leg."

"Instead, we now have a healer for the Elves—that's Sera—and a doctor for the humans." Lindal leaned his shoulder against the window and tried to look superior. "It seems fitting the vampires are left to fend for themselves."

Zack snorted. "You mean, we aren't vulnerable like you and humans," he said shortly.

Lindal just raised his brow. "If you want to comfort yourself with that, go ahead."

Zack rolled his eyes and looked at Beth. "I see you still don't have a name for the whatever-it-is."

"I do. I just feel silly saying it aloud," Beth admitted.

They both looked at her.

She sighed again. They would pull it out of her if she didn't 'fess up now. "I keep thinking about how it's all encompassing, this thing that arranges the trinities and knew the Grimoré were coming in the first place. It's never tried to communicate with us, yet it's using us just the same. It seems to be all over the world. So maybe it *is* the world, battling to preserve itself and everyone on it, any way it can, against the Grimoré invasion."

"The world?" Zack said, sounding amused.

Lindal shook his head. "No, our world is the same. It

has an intelligence, one that arranges things when it needs to. We don't understand it, yet we know it is there. Earth could be the same, stirred from slumber by a threat only it knows how to deal with."

"Earth..." Zack said flatly, still sounding skeptical.

"Gaia?" Lindal suggested.

"Or Terra," Beth added. "Whatever her name, she's on our side and she knows what she is doing."

* * * * *

When Zoe opened the door, Brady pushed his hands deep into his pockets. Awkwardness was coming off him in waves. "Zoe," he said carefully.

"Hi, Brady. Come in." She stepped aside.

He moved into the house and looked around. "You said to come over at seven," he said.

"That's right. Relax, Brady. We're not going to eat you. Cole is in the living room. Come through." She led the way.

Cole got to his feet as they came in. He didn't smile at Brady. "I'm glad you came," he said sincerely.

"You look great," Brady said. "Better than that. Zoe said you had been ill."

"I've been off-color for a few weeks," Cole said. "This week, for the first time, I feel normal again. Almost," he added, with a little quirk of his mouth.

Zoe smothered her smile. The last few weeks had been

stress-filled, as Cole had learned to deal with his new vampire nature and the overwhelming urges and needs that came with it. Zoe's human presence had not helped. It was Declan's undead yet semi-corporeal presence that had the most calming effect on Cole and the two of them had spent most of the last few weeks locked up, talking things through and sometimes physically hashing out Cole's urges.

Slowly, Cole had been able to spend more and more time in Zoe's company without wanting to eat her. The bonding had been mostly responsible for his fast adaptation to vampire life. The bonding...and his drive to be with them both.

"I can't stand not having you both with me," he had declared. "I just got to have the two of you, now I can't...I'm going crazy."

None of that hard fought-for victory showed in Cole's face as he looked at Brady now. "Have a seat," he told him.

Brady stayed on his feet. He rubbed the back of his neck. "I have to confess...I don't remember everything that happened last time I was here. I remember some of it, though and that's enough to make me want to puke."

"You *did* puke," Cole said mildly. "All over the antique Persian rug upstairs."

Brady's face turned bright red. "I sorta remember..." He sighed. "Send me the cleaning bill."

"Already have," Cole replied. "What *do* you remember?"

"I remember…did I take a shot at you? I mean, did I *actually* fire a gun?"

Cole didn't answer. Neither did Zoe.

Brady let his head roll back. "Shit on a stick," he said, with a heavy sigh.

"Sit down, Brady. Sit," Cole said firmly. "Let's deal with this once and for all."

"I don't know that I can sit, all civilized like that," Brady said honestly. "I feel like a jackass."

"You *are* a jackass," Declan said from the doorway.

Zoe held her breath.

Brady spun to look at him, almost wheezing in surprise. His face, still red from his embarrassment, drained of color, turning a sickly gray around the edges. "Declan," he croaked.

Cole moved. Zoe had never seen him move so fast before yet she had seen other vampires moving at top speed, so she wasn't alarmed when she couldn't see him properly. He picked Brady up and dumped him in the armchair. "Told you to sit," he said shortly and went back to his chair.

Brady gulped air, his fist against his chest. He couldn't take his eyes off Declan. "You're alive."

Declan jumped, reappearing in front of Declan's chair. "Nope," he said softly.

Declan gasped again, his eyes bugging. "Oh dear god," he breathed. "I remember stuff from that day. None of it made sense and I figured I was so drunk I remembered it wrong. Strange stuff...." He sounded on the verge of panic.

"Shh... It's okay," Declan said soothingly. He picked up Brady's hand and held it. "Everything's going to be fine."

Brady looked at his hand, where Declan held it. "How can you do that? Aren't you...a...?"

"Ghost? Because of Cole and Zoe and some other things, I'm more than a ghost, now."

Brady's eyes suddenly filled with tears. "Declan," he said hoarsely. "It's so good to see you."

Declan patted his cheek. "I'd say the same about you, big brother, only you've been fucking around with my friends." He moved over to the sofa, where Cole and Zoe sat and sank onto the cushions between them. He picked up Zoe's hand. "I want you to stop contesting my will."

Brady swallowed. "This house belongs to the family. *Your* family."

"Cole and Zoe are my family. My extended family is much bigger than that. You, Brady, Carol and Jess and our cousins and uncles and aunts...you can be part of that, or not. It's going to be up to you."

"If I give up the house," Brady guessed, his voice bitter.

"Hear me, Brady," Declan said, his voice low. "If you insist on taking the house and fighting Cole and Zoe for it, you'll never see me again. If you win and get the house, then toss Cole out, you'll be forcing me to leave, too. Not because I'm that much of an asshole, but because where Cole and Zoe go, I have to go with them. If you send them away, you'll be sending me away, too."

Brady stared at him. He was pulling himself together, thinking things through. "The three of you are together," he said flatly.

"Forever," Cole said shortly. "We're bound in ways you can't understand."

"Try me," Brady shot back.

Declan shook his head. "Not yet. Brady, you've spent your life preserving the family and this town. What if I said that they're both being threatened right now, by forces you can't even imagine?"

Brady stared at him, thinking hard. "The white-faced man. That was real, wasn't it?" he breathed.

Declan nodded.

Brady swore. "He twisted my thoughts up. *Deliberately.* He had me so ready to kill you, Cole…." He shook his head. "That's the threat?" he said shortly.

"A fragment of the threat," Declan said. "Cole and Zoe and I…we're part of the defense against that threat. Work with us, Brady. You know everyone of influence in this town. We can work quietly, arranging things so that no one is alarmed, so life can go on, yet still protect everyone here."

Brady let out a long slow breath. "How?"

* * * * *

When Brady had gone, Declan came back to the living room where Zoe and Cole waited. He was smiling. "I told you he'd be able to handle it."

"You realize he's going to have your mother and every cousin and aunt and uncle here over the next few weeks, to see you?" Cole pointed out.

Declan shrugged. "If it helps convince them the Grimoré are real and the vampeen are coming, I can live with that." He grinned. "So to speak." He picked up Zoe's hand and lifted her to her feet. "You've been very quiet, my love."

She stared at him, her heart beating. "What did you say?"

"You've been very quiet."

She thumped his shoulder, then smoothed her hand over it. It still floored her that she could touch him in that way, that he was solid and real...*almost* real.

"Of course I love you," Declan said roughly. "I have loved you for as long as I can remember. Only now I can say it. At last."

Cole got to his feet and Declan pulled him roughly into the circle of his arms, too.

"You had to die to say it. Ironic, isn't it?" Cole said.

"So did you, you fanged jock," Declan pointed out.

"Do you mind, Cole?" Zoe asked diffidently. It had

been weighing on her mind for a while now. "No one stopped to ask you anywhere in the panic if you wanted to be turned."

"I would have said yes, anyway." Cole shrugged. "Death, or a life undead with the two of you in it? It wasn't even a question for me."

Declan kissed him, then Zoe. "Nor me. I don't know what I did to deserve ending up with both of you. I do know I will spend the rest of my time working off the debt and I'll do it with pure gratitude."

The next book in the Destiny's Trinities series

Book 6 in the Destiny's Trinities series, *Octavia's War*, will be released in August, 2016.

In the meantime, if you like vampires and ménage:

Blood Knot – The Blood Stone Series

To survive they must trust each other. Only…can they?

Winter, a professional thief who can manipulate others' biologies by touch, accidentally "healed" her former partner—and former vampire—Sebastian, whom she secretly loves. Her healing created a symbiotic pairing between them that neither of them wants.

Nathanial, a sexy thousand-year-old vampire and Sebastian's ex-lover, talks Sebastian and Winter into stealing evidence that will expose all vampires to the world. But Nathanial is a puppet-master who doesn't believe in falling in love with humans, leaving Winter unsure of his real feelings for her once he seduces her, or how he feels about Sebastian, the former vampire-now-human whose life he has turned upside down once more.

But the evidence they steal is hot property. The future of all vampires is on the line and others will stop at nothing to get it, leaving Sebastian, Winter and Nathanial with no allies but each other. They must trust each other to survive. Only…can they?

WARNING: This paranormal MMF urban fantasy contains two hot, sexy alpha heroes, frequent, explicit and frank sex scenes and sexual language.
It includes heart-stopping sexual scenes between the aforementioned sexy heroes, ménage scenes, anal sex and the use of sex toys. Don't proceed beyond this point if hot love scenes offend you.
No vampires were harmed in the making of this novel.

[*Blood Drops are short and novella length stories featuring the characters and situations in the Blood Stone series. Droplet sized morsels for your reading pleasure.]

These are continuing characters and storylines. Reading the series in order is strongly recommended.

———

#1 Best-Selling Fantasy, Futuristic & Ghost Romance Amazon Best-Seller
Top 100, Amazon Vampire Romance Best-Seller
Winner, *Coffee Time Reviewer's Recommended Award*
Goodread's "Most Drool-worthy Covers"
Erotic Vampire Book of the Year, *The Romance Reviews*, 2011
CAPA Nomination, Best Paranormal Book of the Year, *The Romance Studio*, 2011

5 Stars - Not only do you get to read a brilliantly written story, but a novel full of different elements that add hard-edged curves, unbelievable circumstances, and overwhelming odds. *Coffee Time Romance & More*

5 Stars - I'm blown away by the experience of this book. There was so much intensity between the characters, the chemistry between Winter, Nial and Sebastian left me panting in places…I emerged with a lump in my throat, tears in my eyes and my heart racing. *The Bookish Snob*

5 Stars - I lost a little of my heart to each of these characters. If you're a fan of hot urban fantasy (and I do mean oven mit HOT), pick up *Blood Knot*, you won't be disappointed. *Alternative Read*

5 Stars - This is one of those hidden gems in the self-publishing world. I haven't read a better love story than *Blood Knot* in a very long time. This one is her best so far. Don't miss it. *The Romance Studio*

About the Author

Tracy Cooper-Posey is an Amazon #1 Best Selling Author. She writes romantic suspense, paranormal, urban fantasy, futuristic and science fiction romances. She has published over 60 novels since 1999, been nominated for five CAPAs including Favourite Author, and won the Emma Darcy Award.

She turned to indie publishing in 2011. Her indie titles have been nominated four times for Book Of The Year and *Byzantine Heartbreak* was a 2012 winner. *Faring Soul* won a SFR Galaxy Award in 2015 for "Most Intriguing Philosophical/Social Science Questions in Galaxybuilding" She has been a national magazine editor and for a decade she taught romance writing at MacEwan University.

She is addicted to Irish Breakfast tea and chocolate, sometimes taken together. In her spare time she enjoys history, Sherlock Holmes, science fiction and ignoring her treadmill. An Australian, she lives in Edmonton, Canada with her husband, a former professional wrestler, where she moved in 1996 after meeting him on-line.

Other books by Tracy Cooper-Posey

* = Free!

Blood Knot Series (Urban Fantasy Paranormal Series)

Blood Knot*
Southampton Swindle
Broken Promise
Vale
Amor Meus
Blood Stone
Blood Unleashed
Blood Drive
Blood Revealed
Blood Ascendant

Beloved Bloody Time Series (Paranormal Futuristic Time Travel)

Bannockburn Binding*
Wait
Byzantine Heartbreak
Viennese Agreement
Romani Armada
Spartan Resistance

Kiss Across Time Series (Paranormal Time Travel)

Kiss Across Time*
Kiss Across Swords
Time Kissed Moments I
Kiss Across Chains
Kiss Across Deserts
Kiss Across Kingdoms

The Kine Prophecies (Epic Norse Fantasy Romance)

The Branded Rose Prophecy

The Stonebrood Saga(Gargoyle Paranormal Series)

Carson's Night*
Beauty's Beasts
Harvest of Holidays
Unbearable
Sabrina's Clan

Destiny's Trinities (Urban Fantasy Romance Series)

Beth's Acceptance*
Mia's Return
Sera's Gift
The First Trinity
Cora's Secret
Zoe's Blockage
Octavia's War
The Second Trinity
Terra's Victory

Interspace Originas (Science Fiction Romance Series)

Faring Soul
Varkan Rise
Cat and Company

Short Paranormals

Solstice Surrender
Eva's Last Dance

The Vistaria Affair (Romantic Suspense)

Red Leopard*
Black Heart
Blue Knight
White Dawn

Go-get-'em Women (Short Romantic Suspense Series)

The Royal Talisman
Delly's Last Night
Vivian's Return
Ningaloo Nights

Jewells of Tomorrow (Historical Romantic Suspense)

Diana By The Moon
Heart of Vengeance

Scandalous Sirens (Historical Romance Series)

Forbidden*
Dangerous Beauty
Perilous Princess

Romantic Thrillers Series

Fatal Wild Child
Dead Again
Dead Double
Terror Stash
Thrilling Affair

The Endurance (Science Fiction Romane Series)

5,001
Greyson's Doom

Contemporary Romances

Lucifer's Lover
An Inconvenient Lover

The Sherlock Holmes Series (Romantic Suspense/ Mystery)

Chronicles of the Lost Years
The Case of the Reluctant Agent

For reviews, excerpts, and more about each title, visit Tracy's site and click on each title in turn: http://tracycooperposey.com/books-by-thumbnail/